W0232763

Pethavan

OXFORD NOVELLAS

Encompassing literature, popular and genre fiction, writers old and new, this series presents an orchestra of Indic voices

Series Editor: Mini Krishnan

Other titles in the Series

Pethavan
The Begetter

Imayam

Translated from Tamil by
Gita Subramanian

OXFORD
UNIVERSITY PRESS

OXFORD
UNIVERSITY PRESS

Oxford University Press is a department of the University of Oxford.
It furthers the University's objective of excellence in research, scholarship,
and education by publishing worldwide. Oxford is a registered trademark of
Oxford University Press in the UK and in certain other countries

Published in India by
Oxford University Press
YMCA Library Building, 1 Jai Singh Road, New Delhi 110 001, India

© Oxford University Press 2015

The moral rights of the authors have been asserted

First Edition published in 2015

All rights reserved. No part of this publication may be reproduced,
stored in a retrieval system, or transmitted, in any form or by any
means, without the prior permission in writing of Oxford University
Press, or as expressly permitted by law, by licence, or under terms
agreed with the appropriate reprographics rights organization.
Enquiries concerning reproduction outside the scope of the
above should be sent to the Rights Department, Oxford University
Press, at the address above

You must not circulate this work in any other form
and you must impose this same condition on any acquirer

ISBN-13: 978-0-19-945952-0
ISBN-10: 0-19-945952-5

Typeset in Berling LT Std 10/15.6
by Excellent Laser Typesetters, Pitampura, Delhi 110 034

To all those brave women and men in
Tamil Nadu and elsewhere who are
fighting against atrocities perpetrated
in the name of caste and community

CONTENTS

Series Editor's Note

The Oxford Novellas, the first series of its kind in English translation, assembled from different Indian languages and from different periods in time, are now more than a year old and have received some attention and respect from the reading and reviewing community.

Much longer than a short story but much shorter than a full-length novel, the novella has lived in the shadow of its cousins for a very long time since its formal shaping in the nineteenth century and is a vehicle which permits experiments with style, register, location, and character without appearing crammed or cramped.

Having published plays, poetry, life writings, short stories, novels, and travelogues in the Oxford translations programme, we felt the need to present this neglected genre in a selection of intense fiction offering arresting insights from different Indian languages. Our explorations led us to a great range of cultural characteristics embedded in this form reflecting the tensions and anxieties of our civilization, our hope for equality, and for retaining our humanity in contemporary Indian society.

In 2013 we launched the series with six novellas, this year we added a few more from Konkani, Tamil, and Malayalam.

It might be remembered that different centuries coexist in the contemporary reality of the country. The Indian-language writer, inheritor of a stupendous history, both fed and buffeted by outside-India influences, might choose a rural theme with its near-medieval ambience but handle it in very contemporary language.

Linked with artistic excellence (as far as the engineering of this project is concerned) is the fundamental importance of translation in expanding literary domains particularly in a country where this linguistic and cultural process constitutes an important mechanism of its evolution. Building a sense of oneness in the Indian psyche where none existed till very recently in its very long history, is one of the by-products of any contemporary translation venture. Commerce, colonialism, and cultural allure have built the overpowering prestige of

English, the passport language to a wider readership both within India and outside it.

Avoiding an aggrieved nationalism and keeping in check an anti-West aggression that so often tinges discussions and articles about translations into English, it would be interesting to study the strategies our strongly bilingual and bicultural translators use to convey experiences and sentiments unique to India. A comparison of the English used by Indians who write only in English (since they cannot express themselves in their mother tongues) with the English forged by Indian translators into this same language, should offer a rich study and historical record of the growth and shifts in the development of English in our postcolonial context. As Nicholas Ostler said, 'Shared language is what binds any community together and makes possible both the living of a common history and the telling of it.'

MINI KRISHNAN

A Story Written by Society

The three novels, *Koveru Kazhuaigal* (1994), *Arumugam* (1999), and *Chedal* (2006); the four short-story collections, *Manbaram* (2004), *Video Mariamman* (2008), *Kolai Chaeval* (2013), and *Savu Soru* (2014); and this one novella *Pethavan* (2012) are my literary accomplishments till date. Many expect me to tell them how I wrote these books, but I find myself unable to fulfil their expectations. A 'trader' needs to provide what 'sells' in a market. I am not a trader; I am a writer. The quality of literary output lies in its authenticity, not in the number of people who read it.

The question *why* I produced these works is far more important than *how* I wrote them. I write because it makes me contemplate society and the human condition. Writing makes me ponder over social issues with care.

I have certain questions and criticisms about the society in which we live, against its psychology, against its social and cultural values, and about its system of justice. This is the substance of all my writings.

My intention is to raise questions. Raising questions and the quest for answers form the basis of writing; not providing all answers or conclusions or solutions. Giving shape to the questions and criticisms that lie deep within the recesses of society's conscience and establishing it on the foundations of truth are the essence of my writing. The writer need not talk about, or defend, his writings. Once the work is done, the relationship between the writer and his writing ends. I have no place in the universe that I have created. Thereafter, I too am just a reader. My writing aims to achieve silent introspection, and not agitation.

Why is life not the same for all individuals in a society? Why is human life—which should be wonderful—as degenerate as it is? What is the relationship between me and my fellow human beings? What is this enmity among us? What leads to recurring contradictions? Who am I? What is the world? What drives the kind of emotions that lead one to say that 'the world is nothing', 'life is nothing', and that 'everything is a farce'? Why does the world continue unchanged, despite its many religions, preachers, and even after the appearance of many social reformers and moral philosophers? Why does society, why do social institutions, lack ethics and morals? What causes apartheid, discrimination, disparities, and economic exploitation to continue across the ages? What are the boundaries of human needs and wants? What is culture? What is tradition? What is true happiness and true sorrow? How do people manage to face their lives in this cauldron of suffering? What is the force that still moves humanity forward? Questions like these, and thousands more, are brought to life in my writings. That is all. My writings do not provide answers, or conclusions, or solutions; they only raise questions.

This place where I was born and brought up, the people who live here, their way of life, the rules and regulations of this place, the ethics, the morals, the conventions, the beliefs, and traditions—this is my life. This is my creative universe. The characters of *Pethavan* emerge from here.

My characters are not great thinkers or rebels. They belong to the land. They are labourers. Theirs is a constant struggle with land and nature. Labour is their strength. That is what makes them struggle with nature. They do not have big dreams, wishes, goals, or expectations. Their life is all about managing the means to keep hunger away. All their lives they struggle to fill their plates. But they are used to losing that battle all the time. My characters do not even dream. Even if they dream, it is about eating well. For them, life revolves around their stomachs. They live their lives the way it happens. Like them, their needs and desires are also simple. The sheep should give birth to two lambs, the cow should give birth to a calf, the pig to piglets; and with the money earned from that, the good and bad in life have to be managed. Above all, there should be rains and a good harvest of grain. This is what they desire more than anything else. Their most intense prayers are for food, to fill their stomach and a little bit of cloth to keep their human dignity intact. Nothing more. What does a human being need beyond this? They do not fit into the moral and ethical constructs of Tamil society or Indian society. They are the subjects of ridicule, insults, and humiliation. But how have these disgraceful characters—the subject of ridicule, and the symbols of depravity—become stories that are respected by Tamil society? How did they become mirror images of the Tamil way of life? None of my characters were created by my mind. These characters are still walking in front of my eyes. The characters of *Pethavan* are no different. Literature is neither removed from nor alien to life.

Has any woman said that becoming a sex worker is her life's goal, her dream? Without desire, and against their wishes, how do women continue to be converted into sex workers? Whose choice is this? Has anyone ever said that becoming a thief is my desire, my dream? How is it that some people are forced into becoming thieves? What compelling social factors lead to such situations? Why have all the so-called morals, be it caste, religious, social, or even traditional and cultural values, and honour been woven only around the idea of 'the woman'? Why does this practice still continue? The love story of Bhakkiyam in *Pethavan* becomes a matter of interest everywhere. Village panchayats discuss it. The 'caste' talks about it. The 'party' talks about it. Who decides Bhakkiyam's love … life? Did Bhakkiyam reach her lover after the bus journey, or was she murdered on the way? I do not know.

The characters in my story are those who have accepted the life destined for them without any complaints. They never questioned why others—society—determined their lives. But they live their lives with passion, complete involvement, and to the fullest. They never consider their lives as low or mean and never look upon it with disgust. They never blame anybody for it. Only hearts with desires have these characteristics. The protagonists in my story live their lives. They express themselves in their own language. They convey the story of their lives to me through their tears, through words, and through their songs of lamentation. These have formed the basis of my novels and short stories.

The characters in my stories were part of real events. They faced social realities. They are witnesses to how Tamil society lived in a particular place in a particular period of time. I have only chronicled the lives of the witnesses who bear testimony to the way Tamil society lived. They live: animated witnesses who determine what literature is and who is a writer. My protagonists do not ask for money, gold, bungalows, car, or sex. Only rice. But this society has refused to give even that to them. And so they have to struggle.

Why should a girl's story, a family's story be written? Did they lead a life that was totally different from that of everyone else? History does not give importance to an individual's or a family's life story. On the contrary, it is the story of a society that should be written. That is the life of a place—the life of an era. I write a story to record the contemporary state of society—to describe how society was in a particular period of time.

Characters such as Pazhani and Bhakkiyam helped me preserve their contemporary social realities by articulating it in their own words, creating a language entirely their own. They showed me the way and acted as mirrors to reflect the images of the time.

I never impose myself on the nature of the characters, or their language, nor do I have any special attachment towards any of the characters. While a writer should be close to the lives of his characters in entirety—taking in both its positives and negatives—he also has to stand apart from their lives for an objective view. I want to perceive and project a scenario on its own virtues. All kinds of restrictions, boundaries, definitions, and principles, including all sorts of 'isms', only impair a literary work. Neither I nor my writings suffer from this deficiency. Literature should articulate the centrality of human relationships—with a minimum of words; if possible, without any. That will allow space for all kinds of interpretations. My writing is just an articulation of the words life provided and the reality those words conveyed.

The purpose of my writing is to make an attempt to comprehend all the greatness as well as all the shame associated with human life; the moments when human beings lose against nature and all the emptiness surrounding life.

This novella is just an answer to the questions I constantly ask myself. *Pethavan* is not a story authored by me—it is a story written by society itself.

I thank the translator Gita Subramanian for her effective translation, Ambai for giving an incisive introduction, and editor Mini Krishnan for her deep interest in the story and bringing it out through Oxford University Press. I also wish to thank N. Sivaraman, R. Azhagarasan, Gokulvannan, and Antony Juno Jesa.

My sincere thanks to S. Ramakrishnan (of Cre-A Publishers) who helped me fine-tune the Tamil version of the story.

IMAYAM
(Translated by J. Antony Juno Jesa and Gokul Vannan)

Translator's Note

This little gem, *Pethavan* (The Begetter) was brought to my attention by the eminent writer, Ambai. She told me that it was a work of great topical relevance, that it was important to ensure it reaches the largest possible readership, and entrusted me with the task of translating it into English.

Translating this work has been a very emotional experience for me. I had no idea that such 'honour' killings were common in many villages in Tamil Nadu and believed that it was only the male-dominated *khap* panchayats of the north that pronounced such decrees. That this practice prevails in the south as well, and that our women are equally bloodthirsty in their passion to keep the purity of the caste lines, were revelations that shocked me. The first draft of the novella was translated at a furious pace; it was almost as if I had to simply get it out of my system.

When I first read the book, I thought that it would be very easy to translate because of its length. But as I started working on it, I gradually realized how difficult the task was going to be. The author sets the stage to help us understand the fraught atmosphere prevailing in the village almost entirely through dialogues; it is as if any description of the emotions of the protagonists would be an unnecessary diversion from the main events of the story. There is a sense of urgency in every line. To convey the tone and import of the spoken words was extremely difficult, especially as all dialogues are in the local dialect. Though I did manage to produce the first draft in record time, it required numerous redrafts to get to something that I was satisfied with. I realized that it is impossible to translate the effect of dialect and decided that simple, straightforward language was the only option for the translation of the spoken word—any use of common English colloquialism or 'Indian' English detracted from the seriousness of the original by intro-ducing an unintended element of comedy.

One day, quite out of the blue, I got a call from Mini Krishnan of Oxford University Press (OUP) telling me that OUP would like to make this a part of a series of novellas that they were publishing. Ms Krishnan also suggested that I should work face-to-face with Imayam, go through the original in Tamil with him, and compare it with my translated version. We managed to get together in the first week of May and, were in this endeavour, ably assisted by Dr N. Sivaraman, Head of the English Department (Retd), Thiagarajar College of Arts and Science, Madurai. As Imayam read the story out loud, I found my eyes brimming with tears every now and then. When we were close to the end of the session, I told Imayam how moving the experience of listening to him, reading his own words, had been for me. Imayam put the book down and, for a few seconds, remained silent. His eyes glistened. Then, when he tried to pick up the thread again, he choked and could go no further. We had to pause for a few minutes and talk about generalities before the work could continue. I realized a universal truth at that point: the intensity of the emotions the writer feels is what translates into an emotionally charged work such as this. No amount of clever crafting can substitute the kind of passionate repugnance that Imayam feels against this barbaric practice of preserving caste purity through murder.

I would like to thank the following people: Ambai for asking me to translate this work, Imayam and Dr Sivaraman for coming to Bangalore to help me edit my work, and, above all, Ms Mini Krishnan for editing my first draft so thoroughly that all the rough spots were ironed out by the time I incorporated her suggestions and made the alterations. I have worked with other editors, but this experience was an eye-opener for me as none ever went through my first drafts like she did. Thanks Mini, for all the encouragement and help.

GITA SUBRAMANIAN

Bloodied Mirrors

I have known Imayam for many years now. Both as persons and as writers we are total opposites, and yet I have felt very close to the women and men he has created in his stories. His characters have a way of drawing you into their lives, their struggles, their loves, and their language. I have often joked with him that I have learnt all the bad words in Tamil from his characters. But, when they utter these it seems natural for them to speak so.

In the complex web of relationships that he creates in his fiction, it is not the spoken but the unspoken, the unarticulated, the unexpressed that lies underneath like some wounded animal—pain throbbing through its veins and holding onto life—that tells the real story. He has said in an article that his writing is about words that life has given him and life that words have created.

He has also said that he does not want to enter into his characters and speak for them, and that he is not particularly fond of any of his characters as individuals. This is because, according to him, a writer must look at life at close quarters with all its pros and cons, but also know how to observe it and maintain a distance. As a writer, he would like to see the reality around him in a spontaneous, unbound manner for he strongly believes that rules, borders, limits, theories, and 'isms' would only deform a creation. His writing, he says, is not hindered by any of this. He is of the firm view that literature must deal with the core of human relationships, with minimum words, and, if possible, with silence which would convey more than words. He feels that only literature that can deal with both words and silence would create the space for varied readings.

Reflecting on his story *Pethavan* he has said:

The objective of my writing is to observe the glories and degradations of human life, to know the moments when human beings succumb to nature, and to understand the emptiness of life. Along with the reader, I would also like to raise some questions about life and society looking at the way life is and life happens to be. The novella *Pethavan* is the answer to one such question; it is not a story I have written, rather it is a story written by society.

Pethavan was published in the magazine *Uyirmmai* a month or two before the Divya–Ilavarasan love story was turned into a sensational one by the Tamil newspapers and was probably inspired by many such previous, similar, but badly reported or under-reported incidents where an upper-caste girl who marries a Dalit boy was mercilessly raped or killed by her own family, or the couple was lynched by an upper-caste mob. In his usual style, Imayam does not go into any details or explanations. He goes directly into the tense and rage-filled occasion when Pazhani, the father of the girl Bhakkiyam, is standing in the village square being humiliated by an angry caste mob which is jeering, taunting, and insulting him for not being man enough to kill his daughter on the three occasions the village had asked him to. Everyone is raging, including the women.

Very subtly, Imayam makes the unwritten comment that caste violence has no gender. During the angry dialogues that take place at this time, a woman with a baby on her hip tells Pazhani how to kill his daughter and be done with it smoothly and successfully:

> You should pour pesticide down her throat and lock her in a room. However much she screams or shouts, don't open the door and don't give her even a mouthful of water. In a very short while the story will be over.

Imayam uses the common term '*kuzanthai*', meaning child, a baby, to refer to the child at the woman's waist. He does not specify its gender. Maybe the child is a baby girl watching the happenings through innocent eyes and probably sucking her thumb or pestering her mother to give breast; a child who also awaits such a horrendous death at the hands of her own mother who, now so tenderly, holds her at her waist. It is these probabilities which remain unsaid that continue to gnaw at your heart.

The physical appearance or thoughts of the women in the story—his wife Samiyammal, his mother Thulasi, his eldest daughter Bhakkiyam, and his younger daughter Selvarani, who has to drag herself around because of her polio-affected legs—are never described at any point in the story, which is typical of Imayam's way of writing. But, from the events unfolding and the words being exchanged, they come alive in our minds. The frenzied crowd speaks of Bhakkiyam as if she is an animal in heat, but, her grandmother, Thulasi refers to her as a tender banana plant that should not be destroyed.

As Pazhani enters the house, the author says, Bhakkiyam lay in a corner like an 'uprooted' pumpkin plant. An animal in heat in the eyes of the hatred-filled mob becomes a metaphor for two different life-giving, nurturing plants for Imayam. We can visualize the grandmother who begs the son not to kill Bhakkiyam and who rightly points out instances of men marrying lower-caste women and not being questioned; and who asks why only women must be punished for making a choice—the mother Samiyammal, who cannot even bring herself to embrace her daughter when she puts her head on her lap weeping before leaving, and Selvarani who wants Bhakkiyam to live. The women in this story are caught up in a plot not conceived by them in which their roles already seem to have been written. Yet, they try to resist and struggle to overcome their circumscribed roles. We can feel every palpitation of their heart as if it is our own and experience every physical gesture they make. Whether it is Bhakkiyam placing her head on her father's chest and weeping, telling him she does not want to leave him, that she needs him; or Selvarani dragging herself to give more water to her sister, suspecting her father may have mixed poison in the food; or the grandmother falling at the feet of her own son, begging him to show mercy to his daughter; or the emotionally frozen wife who, in the past, had beaten Bhakkiyam mercilessly when, on several occasions, she had tried to run away, and who had not yielded even when the mob once caught hold of her and cropped her hair; or Pazhani himself embracing his lame daughter placing her head on his chest even when he utters the harsh words that he had one daughter with wandering legs and 'a second who can't walk at all'—and each gesture weighs as heavily as a stone on our heart.

The animals in the story stand apart from humans who seem to exist with no humanity. The bullock licks Pazhani's face and calms him down. He allows his face to be licked by the bullock and, slowly, his trembling stops. His dog hovers around, concerned and unwilling to leave him in this trying moment.

It is not easy to forget these women, the man Pazhani himself, and these animals which are part of their lives. In a talk he gave at the Manonmaniam Sundaranar University on 4 March 2013, Imayam spoke about the women he has written about. Imayam claimed in the lecture, and has generally given the impression, that he is a male chauvinist like many other men, and that all the negative qualities assigned to men by Tamil society regarding women reside in him too. And he is himself surprised that his stories have women as central characters. They came to him not as characters but as narrators of history, of a society, as those who have lived the history of a society, he explains. He differentiates his women from urban women claiming various rights. In this passionate speech Imayam says:

My women are not highly educated. They are not those who speak of women's body, gender politics, politics of the body, woman's language, women's progress, women's existence, or sexual freedom. They don't know English nor are they interested in understanding ideologies or concepts. They are not great beauties. They are not thinkers or revolutionaries who can talk about the society. They do not shout, 'Let male authority be destroyed, let femininity thrive!' or 'Let us avoid motherhood and save womanhood.' My women have come into being through their mouths and their stomachs. And they live with their mouths and stomachs. And they struggle throughout their life to fill their mouths and their stomachs. And they keep losing in their struggles. My women don't even dream. If at all they dream, they dream of having a stomach full of food. That is because the stomach is their life. It is for us too.

My women are not women with ideals nor are they modern women. They are below-average women. Not of high caste and without high qualities. They have no property, no jewels, and no status in society. They are not even beautiful. They don't even have the protection of family, husband, or children. Many of them are widows, old women, and unsophisticated village women. How did they become stories and the symbols of Tamil society? How can women become the identities of a society? These women don't have the moral and ethical qualities assigned to women in Tamil society and Indian society. These are women who have been ridiculed and made fun of by society. How did these lowly symbols of a society become the stories respected by Tamil society?

How did they become representatives of Tamil life? …
These women are created by society, for itself. They are
public property. They are those who have been offered
as sacrifice for the sake of society, created by society.
They have been sacrificed for society's work, its plea-
sures, and its beliefs. And these are the women who have
become what now stands for Tamil society's existence
and they are the cultural symbols of Tamil society today.

Imayam does seem to have very critical views of
women who fight for women's rights claiming equality
and freedom. But if one reads his speech carefully, one
can tell that his attempt is more to contrast his women
characters with not only the rights-seeking women we
are familiar with, but also with the women of the epics—
women like Kannagi—who have become symbols of
a culture. His emphasis is rather on their struggle for
survival and their being manipulated by society in the
name of caste or culture. That is why, at the end of the
talk, he says that his aim is not to write the story of a
particular woman or a family, but that of a society at a
given period of history. His women characters become,
for him as a writer, the mirrors of the society he is
writing about.

Seen in the light of Imayam's very precise and poignant description of his women characters and his writing, one can understand why *Pethavan* is written the way

it is. Imayam chops away all the extra words and retains only those that will make his story pierce the mind like a sharp and painful knife. *Pethavan* is a story snatched from the centre of many happenings. It is as incomplete as many things in life. There is a death which leaves behind women, of many age groups, to struggle on their own. Does Bhakkiyam reach her destination? Or is she murdered on the way? Are happy endings possible in a society that seems to have forgotten that the anti-caste Self-Respect Movement took place on its soil?

I have read *Pethavan* many times, and each time I have cried when the father feeds his daughter, places her head on his chest, and hugs her. His language is abusive and abrasive throughout; but his words, when he bids Bhakkiyam goodbye and tells her to go live her life, make not only his daughter and his future son-in-law, who speaks to him on the mobile, cry, but also the readers. Maybe Imayam is not really the male chauvinist he claims to be, or maybe like most Tamil men he also harbours prejudices against educated, city women who speak a different language. It is not unusual for writers like Imayam, who portray unforgettable women characters, to constantly intrigue their readers with their sensitive stories and their public pronouncements. But *Pethavan* makes one feel that maybe, beneath that rough exterior beats a heart that has understood how women live and die in Tamil society. When a story rises above the public image of the writer, it has truly succeeded in having an existence of its own that goes beyond the writer.

AMBAI

'*On*
our family deity I swear—I won't go back on my word. Tomorrow, by this time, the village will have the news. But not today—Friday!'

'Is this a wedding? Why look for an auspicious day?' asked a young man.

Chains of questions. Pazhani felt he was being churned through an oil press.

'Three times you have not kept your promise. The villagers might soon consider you a good-for-nothing. They have been quiet about what your daughter has been up to, only because *you* are known to be a good man. Just say a word that you can't and we'll take care of it,' shouted Selvaraj from North Street.

'Are we as spineless as him? What a shame, our villagers do not have the same passion as the people from Nallur,' the young man who had spoken earlier said.

'Ask, go on, ask,' Poorasami from Perumal Koil Street egged him on.

'Tomorrow I'll not go back on my word!'

'*Maama*, isn't that what you said earlier as well?' taunted the local politician, Durai.

'Tomorrow, the village will know who Vandikkaran House Pazhani is.'

'Is that so? We believe you; we will take you at your word. But tell me, how are you going to accomplish the deed?' asked Durai.

'As the village says.'

'You should pour pesticide down her throat and lock her in a room. However much she screams or shouts, don't open the door and don't give her even a mouthful of water. In a very short while the story will be over,' said the young woman who held a baby on her hip.

'I will give her Polidol. That won't take very long.'

'This is not some wedding ceremony for a crowd to gather and make a song and dance of. So you finish it on your own, Maama. There is no need for anyone from outside to hear of this. There will be no case or anything. Even if there is, I'll take care of it. Only if we go around talking about it will anyone know what was done. When the whole village is united, how can even a tiny clue slip out? When it is all over, the body should be removed at once. No playing around with it! It should be burnt to ashes. It should not be a repetition of what happened in Nallur,' said Durai with a responsible air.

'Call Athai as well. We should ask for her opinion too.' As soon as Durai said this, three or four boys pulled Samiyammal out of her house.

'Athai, did you hear what Maama said?'

'I did.'

'What do you say?'

'The same as Maama. Bring me a bottle of Polidol. I will turn her into ashes without anyone seeing what happened.'

'You won't go back on your word?'

'Tomorrow by this time the village will know whether I slept with just one man, or with many. I will chop her to pieces.'

'Fine, go now! Are we doing this for ourselves? The thousand men gathered here have to be able to carry themselves with dignity. That's why.'

As soon as Durai said this, Samiyammal went back inside.

'Sit down, Maama, we'll talk about the rest of the arrangements,' Durai said.

'No harm in standing. Speak!'

The crowd started talking about how to take the body out for cremation. The panchayat, that had started when the evening was darkening, went on and on.

'What is this, the whole village assembles and says that we should chop up and kill one of our own children! Will the gods approve? You should get that boy here and rough him up. Or, you should fetch his parents here and give them a sound thrashing. Warn them that we will drive them out of the village! If they do not come round with that, get hold of all three of them, tie them to an electric pole, and skin them alive. Or, parade them stark naked round the village four times. Instead of doing that, what kind of idiotic panchayat are you holding here? Making one of our own kind stand here and questioning him!' When the old man Mandayan from East Street said this, the entire crowd jumped on him.

'You can't see anything and you know nothing, nothing at all. You broke your leg and went off to your daughter's place and returned just today after two years. What do you know of what's been happening here for these past three years? We've beaten up that fellow four times at the Vridhachalam bus stop. Making it appear to be an accident, twice we set fire to his house. In the dead of night, we freed the goats and the cows tethered in his house. Once, we slaughtered two of his goats and ate them. We set fire to his cane fields. We set up caste panchayats and had him fined five times. His parents have been tied up and beaten black and blue; how much more can we beat them? Nothing has worked. Because of all this the village has been smouldering for a whole year. It looks like it is going to lead to a big caste war. But the caste panchayat said, "It has nothing to do with us, really, it is between him and you." Even if he leaves her alone, she won't be. As they say, even if darkness dies, thieving hands will not stay still. She goes after him like an animal in heat. Till a cow has a calf or two, it is going to go scouring the forest and river banks. We have tried to reason with her, both with words and with our hands. The whole village got together and beat her up. Twice, we left her almost dead. We tried chopping off her hair. But even with all that her lust knows no end. Such a shameless cow! And she won't even die! It looks like she will only die after she has shamed the entire caste! Who is going to cry if a creature like that dies!' Selvaraj narrated this to old man Mandayan in utter disgust.

'My, my! Such frenzied desire! In that case, that fellow should be brought here; the two tied up together and then killed!'

'He is a policeman. That's the problem. That's why the story has been going on for three years.'

'A senior police official?'

'A sub-inspector.'

'What does it matter who he is? If he is a policeman, does he think he should have a higher-caste girl? His *paadai* too should be prepared.'

'You see nothing and know nothing! Just go home and sleep. We can continue living here only if her body is taken to the cremation ground.'

'Still, do you have to call the entire village panchayat just to finish off one man? You should have torched the entire street he lives in!'

'Yeah, yeah, we can do all that. You just keep quiet! Don't we need cashew pickers?'

'I don't like your girlie panchayat,' and the old man Mandayan cleared his throat and spat.

'You doddering old fool!' said Selvaraj, staring at him. Then the party man sitting next to Durai said, 'Three times they have failed. Leaving it up to the parents for the fourth time does not seem right to me!' At that, Pazhani's neighbour, Seenu said, 'What you say is correct. Let us not waste time talking about this and that. I too feel that tomorrow is not right. Try to finish it off today itself. Word of this will spread. Once it spreads, it will be very difficult to finish the deed. It won't even take the time to take a piss—just take the sari she is wearing and twist it tight around the neck and hold it—and finished. Then, if you cremate with four kilos of sugar added to the logs, in just half an hour everything will be ashes. Then, gather it all up and throw it into the tank. Only then will the females of this village know some fear.'

'The problem continues only because Maama is such a good man. The plot would have been very different otherwise. Even when our leader asked me, that was why I told him that we would settle it within the village. He too agreed and said "Do it without any outsider getting a hint of it,"' said Durai.

'Why did you tell him about this?' asked Pazhani.

'I didn't go specially for that. I'd gone on some other business. Then the leader himself asked me. He was worried that it might become a problem like Nallur or Paalur. There is nothing wrong with the leader knowing. After all, tomorrow if there is some complication, he is the one we will turn to for help.'

'So the story of my shame is spreading from village to village!'

'Are we responsible for that? It is because of you and you alone that the village has been shamed. You would have been a man if you had killed her as soon as you found out. Okay, if that was not possible then, where was your sense of shame and pride when she ran away three or four times? Okay, let that be, what about the

three times when your wife asked the village panchayat
for more time? Shouldn't you have finished it off then?
Forgetting all that, you have the gall to talk like this
now!' The party man spoke with disgust. 'What kind of
a father are you? Because people like you are born into
our caste, no one respects us any more. Tomorrow, your
daughter's corpse should burn in the cremation ground.
Otherwise, your corpse will. Remember this, does your
daughter think the men of this village are all women? It
is because of one or two whores like her that our caste
has lost its honour in society. Couldn't she find someone
from among our own boys?' the party man gave vent to
his anger.

'Don't be so angry, *mappillai*!' Durai said.

'One girl has made us all bow our heads in shame,
how can we not be angry?' The crowd screamed back
at Durai.

'This time there will be no dithering. If there is, you
can remove your slippers and ....'

After Pazhani said that, the crowd calmed down.

'Tomorrow you are finishing off the job!' said Selvaraj
in an authoritative tone.

'Yes.'

'Who will buy the Polidol?' asked Poorasami.

There is no need to spend village money on that,'
said Pazhani.

'The body will be taken by the village,' Karthi said venomously.

'Whatever … whatever you wish or the village wishes.'

'Tomorrow no one should leave the village.' The party man stood up and announced loudly to the whole crowd. 'No one is to step out of his house even to work in the fields. Anyone responsible for word of this getting out will not be allowed to stay in this village.'

'How will we lift the corpse of a girl who has died a virgin?' Poorasami asked.

'Of course, only after observing all the required rites,' said Selvaraj. At that, an old lady in the crowd said, 'So a wayward creature requires "due rites"? Instead of strangling her, you run a "girlie" panchayat! If this had happened in my native village of Koravankuppam, they would have ended her story the very night they found out about it!'

'What is this "Nallur business" they are all talking about?' old man Mandayan asked Selvaraj who was sitting next to him.

'Two or three years ago there was an incident in Nallur which is close to the town of Vridhachalam….'

'A fight?'

'No, no. Just like Pazhani's daughter, a girl from our caste went from Nallur to study in Chidambaram. A boy from the same village, but from a low caste, was also studying in the same place. Somehow the two of them got together. Their names were Geetha and Ravi. The parents and the others around tried their best to talk some sense into them. But the dogs did not listen. The caste panchayats, the village panchayats could not settle the matter. There was a lot of bad blood between the two streets and regular bloody fights. Because of the two of them the village was constantly racked by violence; therefore, to restore peace in the village, it was decided that the two of them should be finished off. Both sets of parents agreed to this. Even the girl and the boy went along with it. A thousand to two thousand people assembled and killed the two in broad daylight by pouring poison into their ears. The bodies were taken to their respective streets and then to their respective graveyards, and buried.'

'*Adi chakkai!*'

'But three days later, the news leaked out. Policemen surrounded the village. They picked up about a hundred each from the two sides and jailed them. That day, you should have seen, how our caste lawyers suddenly descended on the scene.

Goodness, there must have been more than five hundred of them! Even the town of Viruddachalam was shaken up. But though they exhumed the bodies, because the village was so united in its stand, they could not find any evidence and the case was dismissed.'

'Oh, so that is the story! But anyway, where did Pazhani's daughter get trapped?'

'When she was studying in a college in Viruddachalam.'

'Is this what they teach them in all the town schools?'

'Yes, yes!'

'*Kooru ketta koothiva!* The shameless whores! Why did they bury them? They should have been burnt to ashes!'

'That is why we are taking great care to make sure that Pazhani's daughter is cremated.'

'So, she did not like our boys? Her privates should be churned with a large truncheon. Only then will she be rid of her heat. Because they have been made to sit in the shade of the school house, they go around the village looking for fodder. If we take her to the cashew plantation and beat her up, she will be rid of her heat very easily!'

'We have thrashed her well enough but she still won't see reason!'

'Why did you keep such a girl alive this long and not make dead meat of her?'

'Because we have lost our brains, that's why!'

'What is this girl's name?'

'Bhakkiyam.'*

'Good name! My piss on her face!'

'Tomorrow, by this time, the corpse should be burning.' Saying this, Durai got up and part of the crowd got up with him. But the crowd did not disperse. They stood around Pazhani and asked, 'You will keep your promise, won't you?'

'I will, I swear.'

He kept promising each and every one. Then three girls came up to him and said, 'Because of this little female baggage, should the village lose its honour? Save the honour of the village! Still, it is your wish—do what you want!' The source of Pazhani's anger was difficult to fathom, but he quickly tore off his dhoti and threw it on the ground, and jumped across it, swearing:

'Tomorrow, by this time, my daughter's corpse will burn—or mine will!'

After Pazhani's oath the crowd began to disperse. But every one of them left only after issuing a warning. The last to leave was the party man who said, 'We are not saying this for ourselves. Our caste's honour should remain intact. Above everything else, the party's honour should not be smirched. The females of other villages

* Good fortune.

should also learn about this. Only then will they learn their place, and stay in it respectfully. At least keep your second daughter, the lame child, safe. If she were not lame, she'd probably have outdone her sister!'

'Yes,' said Pazhani.

The young man standing next to the party man said, 'We will take care of everything required for the cremation. Sugar, kerosene, dried leaves, logs, we will ready everything tonight.'

'Go, go and get them ready!'

'No going back on your word! Swear on our village deity!'

Everyone had left. Pazhani stood alone. All the courage that he had shown in the face of all the humiliation he had suffered facing the crowd, drained away. His legs trembled. To disguise the shaking, he gripped the dog that had been standing between his legs and then sat down on the cot.

He looked towards his house and shouted, 'Die the whole lot of you!' Pazhani's mother, Thulasi, who had been sitting outside all this while said, 'A really vengeful village this is! Why can it not burn down to ashes on its own! These females have made my son hang his head in shame!' She rose slowly and saying 'I have to say something to you, my *saami*!', fell at his feet.

'Let go of my legs. Go, go and die!'

'I have to say something to you!'

'*Saniyan*, Saniyan! Let go of my legs! Why do you also want to kill me? Go away!'

'Listen to me, my saami!'

'Tell me and then get lost, but first let go of my legs!'

'Come, just come with me,' she said. Pazhani tried to free his legs, but could not. He kicked Thulasi. He used the choicest words to abuse her. But he still could not get away from her grip.

'Tell me and then get lost!'

'Just come to me, come close to me, my saami,' saying this she went into the house, to the prayer nook, and appeared to be searching for something. She came out and dragged Pazhani to the cattle shed. She lit the camphor she had brought with her and said, 'Promise!'

'What are you doing? You women are determined to kill me! Why don't you just give me some poison with your own hands! I have had enough punishment for the sin of being born as your son!'

She caught hold of Pazhani's hand and extinguished the burning camphor.

'This is a promise. Do not chop off the family's banana tree. One will become a hundred. A hundred will become a thousand. Listen to me. You will live and prosper!'

'Have you gone mad? Didn't you see all the hullaba-loo here? Only if she dies can I live!'

'Before she was born, didn't you pray for a child for twenty long years? Was all that only so that you could kill her with your own hands? Your prayers will be answered for seven generations!'

'Let me die!'

'A female has to die from this house? Let *me* die! Why should an old woman live?'

'Die then!'

'I will die. But you have taken a vow on our family deity. If the deity is angered, your whole family will be destroyed.'

'That destruction occurred on the day she was born! You think it is yet to happen?'

'So what is your decision?'

'Her corpse has to leave the house before sunrise tomorrow!'

'Is that so? Now hear me, if I was true to your father and slept with no other man, if your father was really your father, then your hand should not touch her! I swear this on your father!' Again, holding onto his legs she shouted, 'Kill me! Then drive her out of the village. Let her die somewhere away from our sight! Let not the sin of killing a weak female fall on you, my saami! It is not her death that I am crying about. I am worried that the son I bore will have to bear the enormous sin of it.

Oh God! My son will have to be born a cow or a goat in his next life to get rid of this burden!'

'Let go of my legs!'

'Don't go back on your promise!'

Pazhani wept aloud along with Thulasi. The dog kept circling his legs.

The sound of the cows mooing. Pazhani asked, 'Did you fill their water troughs? Have you given them their food?' When Thulasi said she had not, Pazhani asked, 'What have they done? We survive and eat because of their hard labour. From the day I brought them here, they have not strayed to eat in anyone else's house. They are not like humans. If you ask them to stand, they will stand. If you ask them to go, they will go. Do they have tongues to say that they are hungry?'

The dog ran behind Pazhani as he untied the cows and gave them water. He piled up bits of straw in front of them. The dog followed him everywhere. The red bullock licked his face. It felt ticklish, but he still made it easy for the bullock to lick him by showing his face to it. As the bullock licked him, his trembling gradually eased. He pressed his face to the cow's face. The dog was sniffing at Pazhani's legs. It was a long time before he left the cattle shed. He felt as if he had had a bath.

'Don't go back on your word, saami!' Thulasi said.

Samiyammal came out. When he saw her, he could not contain his tears; he turned his face away.

The dog kept circling the cot that Pazhani was sitting on. Then, without any reason, the dog went out into the street, barked, came back, and licked Pazhani's feet. Then Pazhani got up and went to the street. He came back and stood near the cot. Then, apparently for no reason, he went into the house. Samiyammal followed him. The dog slept by the door frame. Thulasi sat by the dog.

'Turn on the light!'

Pazhani's words did not seem to have reached Samiyammal's ears. Pazhani threw the light switch himself. Like a chick shivering in the cold, Selvarani sat there shrinking into herself. As soon as she saw Pazhani, she burst into tears. Pazhani could not bear to look at the way she was sitting. He looked away. Bhakkiyam lay by the wood stove, dehydrated, like a pumpkin plant that had been uprooted and left to wither away. Pazhani sat on the floor leaning against the wall.

Pulling herself on her thin, shrivelled, limp legs, Selvarani came to Pazhani. 'Why do you cry, *mma*? Will your tears let me rest in peace?' asked Pazhani as he hugged her to his heart. Hearing voices, Bhakkiyam looked up and seeing Pazhani, sat up. Her face looked like corn on the cob roasted on an open fire.

'Serve me rice!' Samiyammal did not stir. 'Serve me rice!' he said again. It did not look as if she had heard him at all. She sat there as if she was numb. Selvarani propelled herself towards the fireplace. 'No, mma, you stay.' He went to the stove and served some rice and curry and placed the plate in front of Bhakkiyam. He brought a small pot of water, and put it down before her and said, 'Eat!' Bhakkiyam gave him a strange look. Then without any indication of what was going through her mind, she turned around and hit herself on the face. Then she hit her head repeatedly against the wall. No one tried to stop her. Samiyammal did not even look her way.

The word 'eat', that Pazhani had uttered, completely shattered Bhakkiyam's mind. That word stirred her mind like a grapnel that shakes the deep waters of a well. This was the first time in three years that he had actually looked at her face-to-face, and that too at close quarters.

It was when she was in her B.Sc. final year that some-one from the village had seen her with Periyasami in a movie theatre and told Pazhani.

'Is what the boy said true?' Pazhani had asked her. She had given a vague answer which itself had told him that it was true. That was the last he had ever spoken to her. Because she had cried and refused to eat food, he allowed her to write the examinations. During the eight days that she went for the examinations, at least a hundred people made it their business to tell Pazhani, 'We saw your daughter with a son of Vavuthan of our village.' Pazhani had instantly started looking for a bridegroom for her. Out of the six men considered, the boy from Kachchanattam was selected and a date was fixed for the engagement ceremony. The night before, Bhakkiyam drank bedbug pesticide and it had cost him more than ten thousand rupees to bring her back to life.

Six months later, he found a boy from Aaladi and decided to have a quick and secret ceremony. When she realized this, Bhakkiyam tried to hang herself. After that, he decided to not even try to find a bridegroom for her. Periyasami was selected for the post of sub-inspector of police and sent for training. One day, during the second month of his training, Bhakkiyam said that she had a stomach ache and needed to see a doctor. Seeing her board a bus to Madras with Periyasami, some local boys beat her up and dragged her back home. In the heat of the same frenzy, they beat up Periyasami's parents. There was a big uproar over this. Pazhani told Samiyammal to tell his daughter, 'Go and die somewhere!' After that he had not even glanced at Bhakkiyam.

When she had tried to run away eight months ago, she had been caught at Mangalampettai. At that time,

Periyasami was beaten up very badly but somehow he survived. The girls who were picking cashew nuts in the plantations had betrayed her. That night Samiyammal thrashed Bhakkiyam with a broom and with her slippers. Bhakkiyam could not walk for a week. Pazhani would go to the fields in the morning and come back only after dark. Even when home, he would spend his time on the porch or in the cattle shed. But when Periyasami's house was set on fire, when his sugar cane fields were burnt, when their cattle went missing—and news of it reached Pazhani's ears—he called Selvarani and said, 'Ask her if she wants me to live or die!'

Two months ago Periyasami had finished his training and joined the regular force. Nine days later, some cart men carrying loads of sand saw Bhakkiyam near the Sadaiyappar temple seating herself on Periyasami's motorbike at four in the morning. They caught her, but Periyasami managed to escape. The whole village beat her up that day. They mixed cow dung into water and poured it down her throat. The panchayat leader's son, Balu, cut off a clump of her hair. When Pazhani heard the news, he tried to hang himself. It was Thulasi who roused the village and got help to bring him down and save him.

Knowing that Pazhani had tried to take his own life, the villagers decided to hold both a village panchayat meeting and a caste-panchayat meeting that same evening. In the panchayat, Pazhani said, 'She is no longer my daughter. Kill her.' From that night the animosity between the Dalit colony and the village streets grew. Violence exploded on both sides.

'Why is she still alive? How many lives does she want sacrificed? Does she know what is happening in town?' Pazhani asked Selvarani before he bought some rat poison and handed it to her. Eight days later, the villagers caught Bhakkiyam just as she was trying to get away from their street. Again, the entire village, both men and women, beat her up. About twenty to thirty young men took off their dhotis and exposed themselves saying, 'This is what you are running after—how many do you want—take!'

That day, the panchayat met during the day and decided to kill her themselves.

Pazhani said that he would do it himself. The village trusted him. He went to Vridhachalam and bought a bottle of Folidol.* He left it for Bhakkiyam to drink and took Selvarani and Samiyammal away to the temple where they lit camphor, offered coconuts, and came back two hours later. When they got back, Bhakkiyam was cooking rice. Pazhani did not eat that night.

---

* A highly toxic and widely available pesticide.

The next day the panchayat met again.

'I couldn't get the poison. No shopkeeper would trust me. One shop was actually closed. But tomorrow the job will be done.' Pazhani said.

No one believed him. Only Selvaraj and Durai said, 'We'll wait for a day.' That day was yesterday and it should have been over yesterday, so today the village had gathered before nightfall, as early as six p.m.

He was asking her to eat, eat now, when he had already sworn after throwing his dhoti on the ground and jumping across it. He had bought rat poison, he had bought Polidol, and he had brought in a stout rope from the cattle shed and left it in the middle of the house to make it easy for her to hang herself. As if to try and make sure that she would kill herself during the day, he had started taking Selvarani to the fields and keeping her there with him. Now the same man had brought her rice and curry with his own hands as well as water to drink. During the panchayat meeting that had lasted for four hours, only Pazhani had been present; but Bhakkiyam had been lying in the hut, listening to what everyone was saying. Now suddenly it occurred to her that perhaps he had mixed poison with the rice. Samiyammal and Selvarani also had the same suspicion. Selvarani began to cry out of fear. Samiyammal told herself that it would be a good thing if he had indeed mixed poison in the food. 'Let there be a good outcome at least in this manner,' she moaned. Tears streaming from her eyes, Bhakkiyam started mixing her rice and curry only after such a thought had occurred to her.

Thulasi, seated by the dog, brought her palms together in prayer.

Pazhani sat in front of Bhakkiyam. 'Don't cry! You should not weep while eating. It is all the result of your own actions. I have done nothing wrong. This is your last meal in this house. Eat!'

At those words, Selvarani began to cry even harder. Her heart was pounding as if she was about to jump into a fire. But Bhakkiyam was eating with relish. The food went in mixed with the tears that were dripping off her cheeks. With every mouthful, Selvarani's agony intensified. She began to sweat in her anxiety that any moment Bhakkiyam would collapse. She began to shake uncontrollably. For the first time she disliked her father.

Pazhani served some more rice and curry. Only Selvarani, in her panic, cried 'Enough!' But Bhakkiyam continued to mix the rice and curry and kept eating.

Samiyammal said, 'We should have left it to the villagers. Then the sin of it would not surround us and follow us. My heart seems to be exploding like cotton buds in the heat of the day.'

'Do you want more?' Pazhani asked.

'No, *Appa*, enough!' Selvarani said hurriedly and moved towards Bhakkiyam. Bhakkiyam continued eating in a natural way, as if nothing was wrong. To Selvarani, it looked as if Bhakkiyam's face was changing colour and that her eyes were fixed in a frozen stare. The food going into Bhakkiyam's mouth looked like smouldering coal. She placed the pot of water closer to Bhakkiyam. She thought that if Bhakkiyam drank a lot of water the poison would lose its force.

'So all the unpleasantness will be over today. At least let the village be at peace. It has been a while since the village slept,' said Samiyammal.

Selvarani sat next to Bhakkiyam and drew her sister's hand into her lap. Pazhani kept gazing at Selvarani's face. He put away the plate and the pot of water.

'Will you eat?' he asked Samiyammal.

'Yes, yes, I must eat, I must eat—I must eat the poison.'

Pazhani went into the inner room of the house. From a wooden box, he took out the sixty thousand rupees that he had stored in a bag. He also brought out another bag secured with a knot. He sat in front of Bhakkiyam and placed the money on the floor. In the other bag, there were three gold chains, two pairs of bangles, a nose ring, and a ring.

He turned towards Samiyammal and said, 'Take off your chain, nose ring, earrings, bangles—everything—and give it all to me.' Samiyammal sat motionless. Only after she was asked seven or eight times did she stir and then she took them off one by one, and flung them down. Pazhani's behaviour stirred fear in her. She knew that if she spoke, Pazhani might say, 'I am going to hang myself, then you and your daughter can stay here!' and leave the room. Fear was eating into her. She felt as if she was sitting on burning embers, her body felt hot and flushed.

Pazhani picked up the jewellery. Then he told Selvarani, 'You too—take off your jewellery' when Selvarani obeyed, handing over her chain, earrings, and nose ring, he put the money and the jewellery in a bag, tied it up, and placed it in Bhakkiyam's hands. 'Here, this is the best I can do. Keep it. Take your clothes. Flee from this house!'

Bhakkiyam looked like she had seen a ghost. 'Get up. I will leave you in Vridhachalam or Ulundurpettai. After that it is up to you; you have to look after yourself. This is all I can do for begetting you!'

Bhakkiyam screamed as if she had swallowed fire. 'Don't make such a noise!' Pazhani said. But Bhakkiyam seemed not to have heard him.

'What is the point in crying now? That boy studied with you. He is working now. The whole village is afraid of him. Even the party man is afraid. But the whole village laughs at you. Everyone in the village has had children. I did too. One with wandering legs and a second who can't walk at all,' said Pazhani as his eyes clouded over.

'When I got married, I was twenty-three years old. Twenty years later you were born as a gift from god. During those twenty years, there was no temple that we did not visit, no holy tank we did not bathe in. Every year we would sacrifice a goat or a chicken at our family deity's temple. I held *pujais* for the gods. Because she was childless, the kind of abuse that your mother got from my mother was just unbearable. Was she the only one who abused her? The village said all sort of things and so did the world.

'When you were born, I did not give you the old-fashioned names of our village goddesses, like Kaththayi, Manjayi, Mookayi, and so on, but I named you Bhakkiyam, a name that no one else in the village had. Now people are talking about us again. It makes me want to pull out my tongue and die. Even suckling babies are saying things about us. The last three years, I did not survive on food. I survived on shit. Well, it is over. It is all over. You have cut off my nose!' He stared at Bhakkiyam and sighed deeply. In a low tone he said, 'Take the bag. Only those who have their dignity intact have a right to live.' He got up, sniffling.

'Appa!'

Bhakkiyam cried and fell at his feet.

'Don't make a noise!' said Pazhani and this made Selvarani and Samiyammal weep.

'Take your clothes, let us go,' said Pazhani. Bhakkiyam lay flat on the floor by his feet. Samiyammal sat with her back against the wall, stuck to it like a gecko. Selvarani, really frightened, kept crying. No one collected Bhakkiyam's clothes, Pazhani himself bundled her clothes into a bag. He also packed her degree certificate. Then he asked her, 'Do you have that fellow's address?'

'Appa, I want only you, I do not want anyone else!' Bhakkiyam's wails would have melted the hardest stone.

But Samiyammal said, 'Your eyes can actually see your father now, after three years? When you were so adamant, like someone drugged, did you not see him at all? Did I give birth to you so that you can spread your legs to a low-caste fellow?'

'Look how she pours kerosene on a burning house!' Thulasi moaned.

On the day a boy from their village had brought the news, 'I saw her with that low-caste man Vavuthan's son'; on the day she said that she did not want to marry and consumed rat poison; on the day when she tried to hang herself; on each of those occasions, Samiyammal had beaten her up and kicked her till she was exhausted. The three times when she tried to run away with Periyasami and got caught; and the three times the village panchayat had met, she had beaten Bhakkiyam with her broom and with her slippers till her anger ran cold and Bhakkiyam was almost unconscious. However hard she had beaten her, Bhakkiyam had not even uttered a single cry of protest.

'I have given birth to a stone!' Samiyammal would say and hit herself on the face. The three times she had run away, when the village had united to beat her up, forced her to drink dung water, and chopped off her hair; not once had Bhakkiyam cried. Even when some twenty young men had exposed themselves to her, not a single tear had fallen from her eyes. Every one of those incidents merely served to harden her further, turning her heart to stone.

'Appa, I will obey whatever you say. I will marry whoever you tell me to. I swear on our family deity. I swear on *Amma*. I swear on my little sister. I swear on you. I swear on my grandmother. I only want you, Appa!' Bhakkiyam howled, like someone grieving over a dead child, or someone crying over a lost husband.

'What will you get by crying now? Good-for-nothing! After murdering someone you are now shedding false tears! You have stuffed your mouth with mud,' but as she said this, Samiyammal was beset by the doubt that Bhakkiyam might really have changed her mind. 'Women's minds waver,' she said. The way Bhakkiyam was crying and the way she had fallen at Pazhani's feet, and stayed there, all seemed genuine. After ten or fifteen years, this was the first time she had cried like a child. Samiyammal began to wonder if what the astrologer had said was indeed turning out to be true.

When they had learnt of the relationship between Periyasami and Bhakkiyam, they had first tried to beat and kick her. Then, twice they had tried to get her engaged to boys they had selected, but those efforts had failed too. Then, as a last resort, Samiyammal had taken Bhakkiyam's horoscope to the Pennadam Ponneri astrologer. As soon as he saw the horoscope, it was as if someone had coached him to say what he did.

'The child born under this horoscope will go the wrong way. She will be the cause of a lot of strife. I wouldn't be surprised if it leads to a police case and litigation. She will act like one possessed for five or six years. After that, it will start receding slowly by itself and things will become normal again.'

Like a small child Samiyammal had asked, 'Isn't there something we can do to remedy this?'

'Will the rain stop if we hold up an umbrella? Is it possible to dam up the ocean? You think this is just a malignant influence of some planet? The sort that can be negated with some ceremonies? No'mma. This is fate! Written by Eeshan Himself. Go! Fate cannot be averted through the performance of some rituals!'

Though the astrologer said this forcefully, and with vehemence, she would not let go.

'Can you not change anything, saami?'

'Can you change the day the child is conceived in the womb? Can you change the day it comes out from the womb into the world? Not possible. This is also like that. This is fate ordained by God,' he said.

When Samiyammal got up to go, he picked up her offering of fifty rupees, betel leaves, and betel nuts. He knotted the betel leaves and nuts into his dhoti but returned the money to Samiyammal saying, 'Buy oil to light lamps in the Siva temple with this money.' Despite that, Samiyammal tried to give him the money but he firmly refused and said, 'I have six children. I have to fill their bellies by selling my words. Just remember, let go of her, let her go where she wants so long as she can stay alive. Do not start a fight … may you prosper!'

Samiyammal wondered if the *peyi* that had got hold of Bhakkiyam and held on for the past three years or so had indeed released her, as the astrologer had predicted. She wondered if that was what was making her speak as she had done.

'Some malevolent planets are torturing my child!' Samiyammal began to cry.

'Keep quiet! Or something bad might happen,' Pazhani told Samiyammal.

To Bhakkiyam he said, 'Let go of my feet!'

'Appa, only today I'm able to see everything. I will marry anybody you choose! Even if it is as his second wife! It is only now that the blindfold has slipped from my eyes!'

'That is no longer possible! This is not a movie. For so many years now, the village—and the world—have been laughing at you. No one will marry you. Even if we sell our property, farms, lands, everything—and offer everything we get—no man will even come forward. This is a caste that will swallow a sword out of sheer cussedness: a man may not even have a loincloth but he will not give up his caste pride. Even if someone does come, you will not be able to live with such a man. Every day, every moment, you will have to walk on fire. I would rather keep the word I gave the villagers than that.'

'Then do so, Appa. I will drink Polidol like I drink water. I will drink it and go lie down in our cashew nut plantation. Or do what you did before, leave a stout rope here, lock me up in the house, and go out. I'll hang myself!'

'*Aiyo*! Aiyo! After three years, she says this! The wretch! My heart burns! There is no god in this village or in the world!' Samiyammal started to pound her own face.

'Amma, I understood only when Appa fed me rice!'

'I am a sinner!' wailed Samiyammal.

When Pazhani said, 'At least in this do as I tell you,' Bhakkiyam dashed her head against the wall and screamed 'Appa!' loud enough to make the village shake.

'Why didn't a cyclone come and carry away this village? My son had to stand with his arms crossed! Why is there life in this cage that's my body?' Thulasi lamented.

'Will we be able to blindfold the entire village?' Samiyammal asked in a pleading manner.

'No one will step out in this cold. Anyway, there are only two houses on this side, past that we will be in the cashew nut plantation.'

'If the whole village around us is in turmoil, where will we live?' Samiyammal began to cry again.

'No time now. At dawn, I have to face the villagers. See if there is a way of getting word to that fellow,' he said. Samiyammal and Selvarani thought he had gone crazy. No one said a word, so Pazhani said to Selvarani, 'You have a phone, don't you? Explain to him how things are here. Tell him to name a spot to which I can take her and leave her.' The three of them gazed at him in fear, stunned at what he was saying. 'What is he doing? Is he even aware of what he is doing?' they wondered.

Pazhani repeated himself a few times. Because no one responded, he dragged Bhakkiyam and Selvarani out. When he came back in, Samiyammal asked, 'Are we doing the right thing?'

'The villagers will spit on our faces. Let them! Nothing new! Have they not been doing so for so many years now? If we worry about our honour and pride, we can't live. Having given birth to this girl child, do we not have to do at least this much? We prayed for twenty years for her. We asked. God granted. Now twenty-four years later, will He forgive us if we say we do not want His gift?'

'But how can we continue living in this village?'

'Where else can we go but to the cremation ground? No one is going to feed us. No one is going to work for us in the fields, or in our home. No one will come even if

we die. From now on, there will only be funerals in this
house. You should die, I should die. Bhakkiyam's story
is over. Then there is this lame child. Nothing good will
happen to her. She will crawl around this house like an
ant till she dies. So what? We do not need anybody. If we
did not have all this property, land, house, and cattle, the
story would have been very different, we could have just
left and wandered off, going wherever we pleased.'

'People will say so many things!'

'That's what their tongues are for. Let us decide that
from today onwards, we are deaf to the world.'

'I feel that what she is saying now is true. We can get
the village together and tell them. We will pay whatever
fine they ask us to pay. Let three or four years go by. We
will take care of the rest later.'

'They will not listen to us. They will do what the
people did to Chitravalli in Paalur.'

'I don't understand. Was it the same as what the
villagers in Nallur did?'

'No this was different. Paalur is close to Vridhachalam
on the road that goes to Chidambaram. There Daruman
Vathiyar's son, Shekhar, from our caste, and Chitravalli,
a girl from the low-caste street of the same village, fell
in love. The girl had studied up to the twelfth standard.
The father pleaded repeatedly with his son. But he did
not listen. Then Daruman Vathiyar spoke to the girl as

well. She did not listen. He spoke to the people on the low-caste street. They did not listen. The boy refused to get married to any other girl. Just as in our village, there was a lot of fighting with violence and arguments for two years. By then, she had become pregnant. The low-caste people held their panchayat and decided that the two would have to get married and insisted that the wedding take place. They threatened that they would go to the police, they would go to the courts, and so forth.

'Daruman Vathiyar decided to adopt crafty means. He told his son, "You can marry that girl. Tell her to come to a particular place on a specified day." The son did as the father told him to and brought the girl to the temple of their family deity in broad daylight.

'There, all of a sudden, twenty young men leapt out and caught hold of the son and tied him up. Then they went to the girl and said, "This is what you were looking for, weren't you? So many of us have come to give it to you," and all of them raped her. If twenty young men rape a girl, what will happen? She died. Some say that she could not bear the shame of it and committed suicide. Some say that they wanted to make sure she would not tell the world of how twenty men leapt on her and that the men strangled her themselves. You remember, those men in the crowd who said, "Do you want only his? Do we not have one?" and uncovered themselves to Bhakkiyam? They are capable of doing anything. We cannot keep a watch on the whole village. Will a house be robbed only if the door is removed?'

'Aiyo, *Kadavule*!' Samiyammal moaned. 'Four years ago on East Street, Thottikuppatharu's son, Mani, ran away with his own cousin, not some distant cousin but his father's own brother's daughter, Mallika. Three years later they came back with two children and now they live in the same house. Weren't they accepted as members of the family? And the villagers do not think there is anything shameful in *that*."

'Whether she was the father's elder brother's daughter or not, she is still of the same caste, isn't she?'

'Shower caste with menstrual blood *Jatiyile chandai thaan oothi adikkanum*—what caste for one who cannot even recognize his own sister?'

'There are hundreds of incidents in a village! As long as we are on the right side, who is going to say anything to us?'

'But in our village there is no sense of dharma or justice!' said Thulasi.

---

* In certain sections of society and castes in South India, marriage between the children of two brothers or two sisters is considered taboo. However, marriage between the children of a brother and sister is not only allowed but is considered the norm.

When Bhakkiyam came back, limp and wilting with mental exhaustion, Pazhani asked her, 'What happened?' Though he asked her many times, she did not open her mouth. It was Selvarani who said, 'We have spoken to him. A boy from his street will wait with his motorbike at the bank of the lake at Mangalampettai. If we go to him, he will take her to Vizhuppuram and see her off on a bus to Madras.'

'Okay, take your bag, there is no time. The whole village is on a wake like Yama, the God of Death.' He picked up Bhakkiyam's bag, gave it to her, and said, 'Go to some place really far away! Wherever you go, you should stay alive. If your property is taken away, you can retrieve it. If your wealth, jewellery, and possessions are taken away, you can retrieve them. But your life you cannot retrieve. Having prayed and waited for your birth for more than twenty years, as your begetter, this is all I can do for you. Now if I die, you will not be there for me; if you die, I will not be there for you,' said Pazhani and drew in a sharp breath as tears clouded his eyes.

'Do you know how old I am now? Sixty-six. Even today the villagers refer to me by my father's name. They have not said of me, "*Chi*, that man!" No one has said, "Are you really his son?" I will not spoil my father's name as long as I'm alive. I am not blaming you for anything. The times are so. The world is so. You know the story of what happened in Nallur, the story in Paalur, the story in Mutlur. You also know that you were born into a caste where they do not worry about sin or crime or bloodshed. You didn't worry about what will happen in the future. You thought it was all a game. Right, come on!' he said and took two steps. Bhakkiyam stood absolutely still, like a dying tree. Seeing her stand thus, he turned back and said, 'What?'

The house was as quiet as one struck by lightning. A sudden thought struck Pazhani and he said, 'Put some sacred ash on your forehead.' Bhakkiyam stood there motionless, as if turned to stone. He turned to Samiyammal and said, 'Why don't you at least send her off with some sacred ash on her forehead?' There was not the slightest movement from her as well. 'Why don't you come?' he called out to Thulasi. 'You do it yourself!' Thulasi could not contain her tears.

'Is she leaving in order to continue our family tree? So that we can light lamps and invite the members of our caste and community home? She has spoilt the name of my house, she has extinguished the lamp in our home, I will not put sacred ash on her!' Thulasi shouted angrily.

He took Bhakkiyam's trembling hand in his, led her indoors, and stood her in front of a picture of a god. He lit a piece of camphor. He told her to pray. But only he prayed. He applied sacred ash on her forehead. The next moment, like a tree that is felled by the wind, she fell, touched his feet, and prayed, 'Buy the poison, Appa!' Tears rained from his eyes. He lifted the supine Bhakkiyam like one would lift a child and pressed her head against his shoulder.

'What is the point in crying now? I pleaded with you hoping you would not go astray. So did your mother. Your grandmother also spoke to you. But you did not listen. You stayed firm. You thought you could tie up the ocean and lift the mountains. Now you weep. When a fruit ripens, it has to fall from the tree. When it falls, does the fruit know where it will fall—will it fall on a thorn, on a stone, or in the gutter?

'I thought you were born to save me from the shame of being childless. If everything is to happen as we wish, the sea will not taste of salt. I went to so many different temples, but only after we went to the Annamalaiyar temple in Thiruvannamalai, were you born. I had prayed for the birth of a child. I prayed that it be born to live. But I did not pray for this.'

'Appa, buy that poison. Or leave me to the mercy of the villagers.'

'I cannot leave you to the villagers. If they do what they did in Nallur, it would not be so bad. But what if they do what the men did in Paalur to Chitravalli?'

'I will stay and look after my sister. I cannot live without her. She needs someone to look after her all her life.'

'Only now she shows her affection for her younger sister! The crafty actress! What is the point in such clarity when you've reached the cremation ground? Unbearable! Why is my body not already in the cremation ground?' wailed Samiyammal.

'First *she* should die.' Thulasi said, pointing to Samiyammal. 'Marrying my son to my brother's daughter was the biggest mistake. If that had not happened, how would this child have been born? Then my son would not have had to face being shamed by the village, community, and the world.'

'Come, let us leave.'

'No, Appa!'

'If you stay here, your life is not your own. If you wish me to continue living, listen to me. I swear this on you. But then it is up to you.' Saying this, Pazhani placed his palm on top of Bhakkiyam's head. Bhakkiyam ran and dashed her head on the door and screamed. Her cry was like the anguish of someone left naked in the middle of the street.

'She says that she will live on without inviting shame on herself. Why can't she continue living with us for the rest of her life? Did I give birth to a child for it to die like this?'

'If I let it be as it is, will the villagers agree?'

'Oh, my god!' Samiyammal began weeping and wailing loudly. Selvarani wailed even louder.

'Don't make so much noise. Everything will go wrong. They might tie me up in the panchayat; the whole town is united like Duryodhana's gang.' Pazhani's words fell on deaf ears, both Selvarani and Samiyammal had not heard anything. Exactly at that moment, the lights went off filling the house with darkness.

'It would be better if the power does not return today. This work is better done in the dark. Why did they switch off the power at this time? It would be a blessed act on the part of the electricity linesmen if they do not turn it on again,' Pazhani said.

He groped around for an oil lamp and lit it.

Samiyammal said, 'The lights going off is a bad omen. Who knows what bad times are about to befall us? Who knows whose body will become a corpse today?'

Pazhani told Bhakkiyam to sit and sat down himself. Bhakkiyam sat close to him, facing him, her legs touching his. He tried not to look into her face.

'Appa.'

For the first time in three years, Bhakkiyam called out to him from the depths of her heart. That word brought tears to Pazhani's eyes. As if to say 'do not say a word', he held a finger to his lips, and placing her head on his lap, he wept as if his heart would break. His crying shocked Bhakkiyam. She cried out in agony, like someone who had fallen into a fire. Her wails made Samiyammal, Selvarani, and Thulasi also cry out. The house was like a house of mourning.

'Buy some meat tomorrow, Appa! We can make a curry and then in the evening buy the poison.'

'It is as if lightning has struck right in my sight and my family is being scorched and burnt black. Why does that sinful young man not die? I don't know how he drugged my poor grandchild! Now the whole village is torturing my son and beating him up. Someone from our own caste has set up house for a low-caste woman in his car garage. He's even had two children with her. This has been going on for at least three or four years. Don't these dogs know about it? Is Vadapathi, where the man lives, all that far? It is only at shouting distance. Not one of these men is man enough to question that. Anyway, if a man does something, it is one thing, but if a woman does it, it is different! Because she is the daughter of a man who has lost his tongue, they are bold enough to come right into the house and give her poison. And they cut off her hair! They lift her sari and look …!' Thulasi went onto name all the women who had strayed from their caste and slept with men from other castes, both from their own village and the other villages around them. The list was endless, like a thread unravelling from a spool.

Bhakkiyam lay with her head on Pazhani's legs. Selvarani also drew close to him. Pazhani said, 'I do not know what made you change your heart.'

'I don't know, Appa!'

'You don't know?'

'No, Appa. If the villagers had not chastised and beat me up, this problem would not have risen at all.'

'If you oppose them and join the enemy camp, who is going to suffer for it?'

'There is nothing in my heart now. Let us just forget the whole thing.'

'You don't understand. It is like termites destroying a fortress. This is your destiny!' After saying this, Pazhani was silent for a little while. Then suddenly a thought seemed to have occurred to him prompting him to say, 'All this money and all the jewellery is not for you to eat meat and rice daily. With this you should study further. You should become a teacher.'

'This is like filling water in a pot with a hole at the bottom,' Samiyammal said.

'Does that fellow know that we are leaving?' asked Pazhani

'He has asked us to give him a "missed call" when we leave,' said Selvarani.

'Then do that. We don't have much time.' Only after he had said this many times, did Selvarani move to go out to make the call. The dog got up to let her pass.

Thulasi next vented her anger on Selvarani. 'The lame girl is no innocent. The two of them have been dancing to the same tune. Together, the elder and younger sisters have caused such trouble for my son!'

'Check if there is any movement outside,' he said. Samiyammal was sitting lifelessly. Pazhani himself got up and went out. The dog went with him. He looked in both directions of the road. Behind the house, in the cattle shed, in the hay store—he looked everywhere. He came back in. The dog went and lay down at the door.

'No need for any light. Put out the lamp!' Pazhani said. Bhakkiyam kept looking at Pazhani's face. Pazhani blew out the lamp. Then Selvarani came in.

'What happened? Did you speak to him?'

'I told him.' Selvarani said without much enthusiasm.

'Up!' said Pazhani and brought a dhoti and gave it to Bhakkiyam. 'Wrap this around yourself. Your sari should not be seen. If someone asks, "Who is there?" don't even open your mouth. No one should hear your voice.'

Selvarani laid her head on Bhakkiyam's lap and started to cry. It had been three years since Bhakkiyam had spoken to anyone in town. She had not said a word to the neighbours or to any of their relatives. She had not spoken to Samiyammal. If Samiyammal wanted to say something to Bhakkiyam, she would convey it through Selvarani. However, on days when some news about Bhakkiyam hit the village and caused problems, Samiyammal would hit her and shout, 'Why don't you die?' After that till the next complication arose, she would not say even that.

Pazhani did not even do that. If Bhakkiyam was at home, Pazhani would spend his time in the cattle shed or the hay store. And if Pazhani was inside, Bhakkiyam would spend her time in the cattle shed or the hay store. Most of his days would be spent in the fields, whether he had any work there or not. He lived in the fields. For the past three years, Selvarani had been a mother to Bhakkiyam. She knew all of Bhakkiyam's secrets. But no one could make her betray her sister even by a single word. When Samiyammal or the villagers thrashed her, Selvarani would massage the swollen parts, foment it with hot water, apply medicated oil, get hot water for her bath—Selvarani did all that and more. Every time Bhakkiyam was beaten up, it would be at least twenty days before she rose again. Till that happened, Selvarani would not be separated from her sister even by a hair's breadth. Bhakkiyam was only a year older. Selvarani's brain was very sharp.

'The strength of a blood bond! The female will has the strength of a peyi.' Pazhani moaned to himself.

'It is getting late.' When Pazhani said this, there came a sound from outside. Panicking, Pazhani went out and looked around; he went around the house as well. There was not a soul around. 'Why start a new complication? This will be a blot on our name for all time! What can they do to our daughter, if we do not let them? We can send her to my elder brother's house.' Samiyammal said.

'They will set fire to the house at night. We will not be able to do anything. In a similar case in Mutlur, a girl of our caste had had a relationship with a fellow from a low caste. In the end, at midday, with the whole village crowded together, they locked the girl in the house and set fire to it. That's why I am saying this. Wherever she is, she should stay alive. That is what all this is for. Don't make a noise. Don't lock the house till I get back. For a few days, do not bolt the door. Leave the little one at your elder brother's place. You don't need to be trampled by an elephant to die. You could even die of an ant bite.'

'Come!' was the last word he said as he raised Bhakkiyam up.

'Till today, I haven't really done anything wrong, Appa! Let us just leave it at that!' said Bhakkiyam.

Samiyammal retorted, 'See, how much she swears! You still don't understand? First the daughter lost it and now the father. My father gave me to a family of lunatics!'

'She is a crazy woman. She does not understand. You come with me. Our plan should succeed.'

'What if you get bitten by some poisonous creature? How many people do you want me to mourn? Why can't you wait till dawn?' asked Samiyammal.

'You shut up. From the day the decision was taken by the village people and the panchayat, there are men who keep an eye on our house, which is something only I am aware of. Some seven or eight young men are going around saying, you are hungry to sleep with a low-caste fellow, but we will do what needs to be done before it's too late. The party man is at the forefront of this. If ten to twenty fellows step on her like they would step on dung and wring out her life, then all four of us will have to die. Friends and relatives are at the forefront of this. Wherever she is, she should stay alive. Isn't that what you want too? Then what? This is the village that cut off her hair to shame her! If she stays here, the talk won't stop. It will only grow. The fights and arguments will not stop. The brawls between the two streets will never end. Our household problem has become the village's problem. Next, it will become the problem of the whole area, and all the neighbouring villages will start taking sides.'

'Drink some water,' Samiyammal said to no one in particular. Selvarani brought a small pot of water. Bhakkiyam gulped it all down like someone possessed.

'Appa.'

'What is it 'mma?'

'Let my *akka* stay with me. I will make sure that she does not go out of the house.'

'God is there to look after you.'

'Yes, he is there in the onions!' said Samiyammal.

'Sit for a while.' When Samiyammal said this, Bhakkiyam laid her head on her mother's lap.

A gecko made a clicking sound twice.

'The gecko is telling us to rest. Appa, let us do what Akka said and let it be!'

'No it is not giving us a sign in support of staying, it is commanding us to leave. Going is the best option.'

'They are all set to destroy my entire family,' Thulasi shouted.

'Take off your anklets and tie them up around your waist. There should not be even the faintest sound. If caught, they will say the father himself aided his daughter in her foul ways. That infamy will not die, even if I do.'

Bhakkiyam did what Pazhani asked her to.

'I am jumping into the fire because I want you to live. Are you going to be born again to me as my child? Tomorrow if you have a child, keep her safe. Tomorrow you should not have to stand with your arms folded in submission, with tears in your eyes in front of thousands of people!' Pazhani's eyes clouded again. 'One oath— you should not die and we should not either. That is a promise!'

Samiyammal pushed Bhakkiyam away, as she was holding onto her and wailing.

'Go!' she said stiffly.

Selvarani crawled quickly into the interior of the house and brought out a clay piggy bank. 'I do not know how much money there is in this. It is two years, worth of earnings for shelling cashew nuts.'

Bhakkiyam bent down and kissed Selvarani.

Picking up the cloth bag in his hand, Pazhani said 'Come!' and went out of the house. The dog stood outside, ready to go. Even the sound of the dog panting alarmed Pazhani. His eyes glanced this way and that, like one demented.

Bhakkiyam came out into the street and so did Selvarani. Bhakkiyam fell at her grandmother's feet. 'My daughter, the village has got together and put an end to my family line.' Thulasi screamed, fit for the whole street to hear.

'You go and tell the whole village!' Selvarani glared at her grandmother.

'It is this land that we earned, not rupees and paisa. Take a handful of this earth. You will prosper. It is this earth that nurtured you all these years.' Saying this, Thulasi picked up a handful of mud and put it into the folds at the end of Bhakkiyam's sari. Bhakkiyam carefully twisted the material around it and, as if it were a precious metal, carefully tucked it in at the waist.

Bhakkiyam affectionately bit Thulasi's cheek.

'Go by the tamarind tree plantations. Go down at the Purakuttai and then move into the cashew nut plantations!' Thulasi ordered.

Bhakkiyam began to walk towards Pazhani who was standing in the street looking to see if there were signs of any movement.

'Lord of the Seven Hills!' said Thulasi, praying with her palms held together.

'If we reach Purakuttai it should be enough,' said Pazhani, his legs trembling.

Pazhani and Bhakkiyam walked as gingerly as if treading fire, their hearts filled with fear and dread. They walked through the cashew nut plantations for more than an hour. Bhakkiyam could not keep up with Pazhani's pace. The dog ran ahead of them.

When they came to the bank of the lake at Mangalampettai, a boy was standing by a motorbike. Pazhani asked him who he was.

'I am Periyasami's father's elder brother's son, Kanakaraj. You know Vavuthan's elder brother, Thoppalan, don't you?'

'You mean the son of the man who worked in Muthusami's house?'

'Yes, *Ayya*!'

'Do you have a phone? If you do, call that boy.'

Kanakaraj gave his cell phone to Pazhani.

'This is Vandikkaran House Pazhani. Who is speaking? ... I see! I have entrusted my child to Thoppalan's eldest son. When will you give me the news of my child's safe arrival? ... In the morning, at eight o'clock? Don't forget! I can't hear you very well. What will you achieve by crying now? Keep up your father's good name!'

'What route will you take?' he asked, giving Kanakaraj the phone.

'It is now four. I'll take her on the bike to Vizhuppuram, where I will put her on a bus. From there it will take three hours to reach Madras. She will be able to get home by seven or eight.'

'Right, then set off! Get going. Drive carefully. Inform your little sister as soon as you reach.' Suddenly a thought seemed to strike him and he quickly untied the silver cord that he wore around his waist and gave it to her. Bhakkiyam pressed her face to his chest, and, like a little child, embraced him tightly and wailed.

'There is no need to cry. Get on the bike.'

Pazhani stood still watching the bike for as long as the light from it was visible.

In the morning those, who went to the fields came running back and said, 'Vandikkaran House Pazhani has consumed Polidol and is lying dead in the fields. The dog is running in circles around the dead body. The whole area is reverberating with its howls!'

'Oh, we are ruined!' shouted Thulasi running towards the fields.

* * *

Glossary

adi chakkai   an exclamation of appreciation like 'wow!'

akka   elder sister

athai   aunt; father's sister; can also be used to address any older woman in the community

ayya   a respectful term of address for another man or an employer

Eeshan   Lord Shiva

Kadavule   Oh God

khap panchayat   village councils in north India that act as quasi-judicial bodies that pronounce harsh punishments based on age-old customs and traditions

mappillai	son-in-law; usually a term of affection used for any male member of the community or family
paadai	funeral bier with poles to be carried by four men
peyi	ghost, spirit
saami	a term of respect lower-caste people use while addressing an upper-caste man
Saniyan	refers to the planet Saturn which is supposed to have a malign influence on human life

About the Author and the Translator

The Author

IMAYAM (V. Annamalai 1964) is a school teacher and has published three novels, *Koveru Kazhudaigal* (1994), *Arumugam* (1999), and *Chedal* (2006), and four short-story collections titled *Manbaram* (2004), *Video Mariamman* (2008), *Kolai Chaeval* (2013), and *Savu Soru* (2014). Of these, his much-acclaimed first novel, *Koveru Kazhudaigal*, won the Agni Akshara Award, Tamil Nadu Progressive Writers' Association in 1994 and the Amutham Adigal Award for Literature in 1998. The English translation of this novel appeared as *Beasts of Burden* in 2001 and that of *Arumugam* was published in 2006 under the original title. He was awarded a Junior

Research Fellowship from the Central Government's Department of Culture, and honoured with a State award.

Pethavan was first published in September 2012 in *Uyirmmai* (Tamil literary magazine). November 2012 saw its appearance as a little book through Oviya Publications TVS, Villupuram, which reprinted it five times in three months. Bharati Publications published the novella in February 2013 and, has since, sold more than 1,00,000 copies, reprinting ten times. It has also been translated into Telugu by Padmanabhan and published by the Thondanadu Telugu Writer's Association.

The Translator

GITA SUBRAMANIAN taught English, English Literature, and History in Hong Kong. She has produced and directed a number of English plays with her students. Married to a Foreign Service Officer, she has lived in Lebanon, China, Belgium, Bangladesh, Poland, and Pakistan before settling down in Hong Kong, where she lived for eighteen years. During her stay in Hong Kong, she was very active in the Tamil amateur theatre scene. She collaborated with friends in writing and adapting plays in Tamil and co-wrote an Indian–English adaptation of Gogol's *Government Inspector* which was staged very successfully.

Gita has three published English translations of Tamil novels to her credit, of which Nanjil Nadan's *Ettu Thikkum Mada Yanai* won the Nalli-Thisai Ettum Award for best translation of the year from Tamil into English in 2010. She now lives in Bangalore, India.

Dweepa

OXFORD NOVELLAS
Encompassing literature, popular and genre fiction,
writers old and new, this series presents an orchestra
of Indic voices

Series Editor: Mini Krishnan

Other titles in the Series

Vaadivaasal (Tamil)
  C.S. Chellappa

Tyanantar (Marathi)
  Saniya

Sheet Sahasik Hemantolok (Bengali)
  Nabaneeta Dev Sen

Jeevichirikkunnavarkku
Vendiyulla Oppees (Malayalam)
  Johny Miranda

Moogavani Pillanagrovi (Telugu)
  Kesava Reddy

Dweepa
Island

Na. D'Souza

Translated from Kannada by
Susheela Punitha

OXFORD
UNIVERSITY PRESS

OXFORD
UNIVERSITY PRESS

Oxford University Press is a department of the University of Oxford.
It furthers the University's objective of excellence in research,scholarship,
and education by publishing worldwide. Oxford is a registered trademark of
Oxford University Press in the UK and in certain other countries

Published in India by
Oxford University Press
YMCA Library Building, 1 Jai Singh Road, New Delhi 110 001, India

© Oxford University Press 2013

The moral rights of the authors have been asserted

First Edition published in 2013

All rights reserved. No part of this publication may be reproduced,
stored in a retrieval system, or transmitted, in any form or by any
means, without the prior permission in writing of Oxford University
Press, or as expressly permitted by law, by licence, or under terms
agreed with the appropriate reprographics rights organization.
Enquiries concerning reproduction outside the scope of the
above should be sent to the Rights Department, Oxford University
Press, at the address above

You must not circulate this book in any other form
and you must impose this same condition on any acquirer

ISBN-13: 978-0-19-809744-0
ISBN-10: 0-19-809744-1

Typeset in Berling LT Std 10/15.5,
at MAP Systems, Bengaluru 560 082, India
Printed in India at Akash Press, New Delhi 110 020

*To the hope that we will learn to
cherish the Earth which has nurtured*

CONTENTS

Series Editor's Note

> 'Freedom is knowing and understanding things
> quite other than ourselves.'
>
> —Anonymous

Writers have always experimented with forms in their search for the best vehicles for their thoughts, moods, and words. While there might be arguments about what length defines the genre, the novella was shaped and recognized in the late nineteenth century as allowing for greater development of theme and character than a short story without being burdened with the demands of a full-length novel.

Our broad goal in assembling the Oxford Novellas, a unique series combining substance and brevity, is to present the least studied genre from one of the world's oldest literary traditions which includes one of the most sophisticated pre-modern poetic theories. At a time when news is entertainment and literature has to compete with popular fiction, two criteria have guided our selections: socially relevant themes for readers who might want to know things quite outside their experience and understanding, and literary excellence. Thus, famous names march with writers few people have even heard of.

Having absorbed words from nearly four hundred languages, English is opulently equipped to interpret and express the cultural energy of the regions it once entered as the colonizer's voice. If, to paraphrase Wittgenstein, the limits of our language mark the limits of our world, we hope, from time to time, through this series, to move the borders of literary enjoyment further and ever further. Translation into English brings together the creative potential of different Indian languages, the special understanding of the world each one of those languages has, and consequently, the distinctive way they carry the memories and histories of those who use them.

The art of story-telling and the art of narration mingle to give us a literary mosaic made possible by translators working to move texts originally written in other languages into English. We believe that the translator is not merely an echo or a shadow, a reflection or a crib, but a fresh, strong supporting voice that conveys both the said and the equally vital 'unsaid' parts of the original into the receiving language.

Mini Krishnan

Author's Note

The problem of submersion of land in the cause of modernization and the ensuing displacement of the local people is something that has bothered me for a long time.

I worked for about twenty-five years in areas connected with the Sharavathi hydroelectric project. In 1959, when Shri S.K. Patil, Minister for Power at the Centre, pressed a button and inaugurated the project, a huge boulder split into a thousand pieces and stones rained on the tin shed where we were taking shelter. Over the next five years, the Linganamakki Dam came into existence. Slowly, the Sharavathi River deepened not regarding the forests, valleys, canals, villages, the villagers and their agricultural lands.

The villagers were compensated with money and land elsewhere. I have seen people dismantling their homes, loading their extended families and their belongings onto lorries and bullock carts, and going away to wherever land was allotted to them. But who helped them cope with their grief and fear, having to uprooted themselves from everything familiar, from a way of life based on a value system they had known for generations? Nobody thought of that. On the other hand, crafty government officials exploited these people who were ignorant of the ways of the outside world. They sought bribes, they harassed and cheated them.

I poured my sorrow at their plight into *Dweepa* (Island). It is the story of a man who is forced to lose his community identity and fails to cope with his new-found individuality. I also wrote three other novels based on different aspects of the theme of displacement: *Mulugade* (Submersion) which won a prize in the Ugadi issue of *Sudha*, a weekly, in 1983; *Oddu* (Dam/ Barricade); and *Gunavanthe* (A Worthy Woman).

Dweepa came out in 1970 in *Prakasha*, a weekly from Manipal. The late K.V. Subbanna, founder of the world famous institute for drama, Ninasam, was interested in making it into a film. However, in 1978, he said, 'I am not sure if I will be able to make it into a movie but I will publish it through Akshara Prakashana.'

That is how it was published in his press for the first time. Later I was happy to hear that Subbanna had given the story to his nephew, Girish Kasaravalli, to explore its potential for a movie. The film version of *Dweepa* won the President's Gold Medal in 2006 besides many other awards. The novella was published again in 2004 by Ravindra Prakashana together with an article by Girish Kasaravalli and a few stills from the movie.

I am happy that *Dweepa* has now been translated into English. The tragedy in the lives of these innocent victims of modernization will now merge with the groans of the oppressed the world over, wherever this story is read. It is a fitting way to perpetuate the memory of those who lose all they hold dear wherever the country develops at their cost. It is also a proper way of mourning what we have lost because of what we have gained.

My thanks are due to the late K.V. Subbanna and Ravindra Prakashana who have made this story available in print, Girish Kasaravalli and his team who made the award-winning movie, and Mini Krishnan, my editor. Mini is not only a committed editor of repute but also a visionary. In showcasing the plight of the less fortunate in our society through translations of regional literature, she is striving to bring about a social change for the better that includes them. I wish her efforts every success. I thank Susheela Punitha for translating *Dweepa*

into English and for the profound discussions we have
had about the text over the phone.

NA. D'SOUZA

Translator's Note

I learnt about the need for elaboration in translation while translating *Dweepa*, a novella with eloquent silences, the silence of the voiceless and the silence of the stifled. The silences spill over to the reader to stay on after the reading is done. What can one *say* about bonded labourers being bundled out like commodity to be rearranged wherever their masters may resettle? Or about displaced village communities being socially regressed in the name of progress and development? Silence alone can provide the space for introspection and grief.

But to a translator, reading is not a passive skill. She is actively looking for ways to transfer the impact of the original into English, to translate the meanings embedded in the silences that follow cryptic expressions. And she learns the principle behind elaboration first-hand. For instance, take the case of the bonded labourers, Hasalara Byra and Hala. In Kannada, one word is sufficient to describe the anguish of their social condition: *huttaalugalu*. A pause after the word is, perhaps, all that a reader needs to make the necessary cultural and social connections with their plight. But translating it into English literally as *labourers from birth* would puzzle a reader unaware of a social system in India that could withhold the basic right to freedom from a person and his progeny in the guise of helping him out in an emergency. A pause would follow the expression, no doubt, but it would be vacuous with perplexity, not pregnant with grief. The connotative value of the expression required an extended explanation in English: *They were bonded labourers; bonded from birth to their masters as repayment of debt owed by their father*. I was uncomfortable with the verbosity until I realized the elaboration was necessary to fill the silence that follows it with meaning. And in English the pause can stretch to make time for the significance of the social condition to sink it in. Further elaborations in the translation blended seamlessly with the original text, until the story reached its final crescendo in a stifled scream.

Once I came to grips with the theory of elaboration through a hands-on experience with the process, I was happy to use it in place of cumbersome footnotes to ease the flow of the narrative. And I knew my editor, Mini Krishnan, would be happy too, for it was she who had suggested that I should work the meaning of expressions into the context to keep the footnotes to a minimum. I am grateful to her for her meticulous care in reading the text and pointing out turgid phrases that had to be reworked. I am lucky that she cannot read Kannada and does not take certain meanings in the text for granted as I do as an insider! She has helped to make the story in English more lucid. My thanks are also due to Na. D'Souza for reading every chapter as I sent it to him, checking it for the transference of flavour and of details of the historical situation he has presented in the story.

I thank Rajendra Chenni and V.S. Sreedhara for their invaluable review of the text. I thank Chenni especially for his insightful comment that the descriptions are the story. This translation would not have been possible without our collaborative effort.

My special thanks to my family. My husband, children, and grandchildren have been a tremendous support in this venture.

SUSHEELA PUNITHA

Introduction

Dweepa is one of the few novels in Kannada that has development-induced destruction as its central theme. In fact, its author, Na. D'Souza is known in Kannada literary circles as a 'submersion writer', a reference to the many stories he has written about people and families affected by big dams. It is equally important to note that he wrote about the travails of displacement created by the construction of big dams much before 'development' became a matter of prime concern, and a focus of critical attention by social activists, policymakers, and writers. Of course, it has become a universal mantra of progress in contemporary Indian politics and is used as a cover-up to usher in neo-liberal policies, structural adjustment programmes, and even communal violence. At the same time, it has led to various social movements and protests with issues ranging from environmental protection and livelihood questions to upholding human rights.

However, none of these issues occupied centre stage, as they do now, when *Dweepa* was first published in 1970 in the special issue of a weekly. (It appeared as a book in 1978.) It was a time when the growth model had not reached today's menacing proportions and India still looked forward to more developmental work. Though there was widespread disillusionment with the Nehruvian model of progress, the criticism was mainly against the dynastic rule and the monopoly of Congress. The growing sycophancy in the Congress and a marked deviation from the promised path of socialism were considered the main threats to democracy. It was a time when to be a modernist writer meant a refusal to accept traditional values and to look for authentic experience. It is interesting to note that the advent of literary modernity in Kannada coincided with this disillusionment with Nehruvian policy. Poet Gopalkrishna Adiga, who is seen as a harbinger of Kannada modernism, even wrote a poem titled 'Nehru Never Retires' which critiqued the hypocrisy of the so-called high culture. The anti-Nehru sentiment also permeated the thought and writings of the three major modernist writers of that time, U.R. Ananthamurthy,

P. Lankesh, and Poornachandra Tejaswi, in spite of their different approaches to modernity. All of them were equally influenced by Mahatma Gandhi and Ram Manohar Lohia, and shared a common disbelief in Marxist thought. However, their critique of the Nehru era was directed not so much against his model of progress as against the misrule and an abandonment of socialist concerns. The growing schism between promise and performance in the polity found its literary expression in the form of a search for an authentic self coloured by a sense of disquiet, together leading to an exploration of new values. Thus literary modernism in Kannada was constituted by an angst borne by a struggle to cope with life in all its complexity.

Overall, it can be said that Kannada literary modernity was characterized, among other things, by its portrayal of a fragmented self, caused mainly due to fractured democracy resulting in a sense of alienation. Its major concern was to develop a critique of a fossilized culture that was insensitive to the plight of the common people. However, it is important to note that these writers, at that point of time, did not see fragmentation as a handiwork of the new model of development, based on greed and unlimited exploitation of natural resources. It is only later, particularly after the 1990s, that we see Kannada writers, especially Ananthamurthy and Tejaswi, develop a critique of the ideology behind the new model of progress and development in their writings. While the former turned to an exploration of the pre-modern self, the latter took to environmental forces as a means to explore the unknown modes of being. Tejaswi's writings repeatedly point to the perils of environmental degradation and the loss to human life caused by our unlimited plunder of Earth's resources. This shift is understandable as it reflects a growing pan-Indian concern for protecting nature from human greed, thanks to the advent of several important and influential gender- and environment-based social movements which gathered momentum during the late 1980s. These movements opened new ways of conceptualizing the world and unleashed new ideas related to the question of 'being in the world' with a force that no writer could ignore.

Meanwhile, literary modernity in Kannada had undergone a shift. By the 1970s, it had lost its force, thanks to the rise of various protest movements like Bandaya and Dalit, resulting in the awakening of a new social consciousness that questioned the excessive preoccupation with the insulated individual self of the modernist era. The evidence of an awakening of Shudra consciousness in literature was already evident in writers like Kuvempu, but it was framed within a broad liberal humanistic outlook. The new Dalit-Bandaya movement, however, was different in the sense that it drew the active participation of writers from the marginalized communities and was even supported by early modernist writers like Lankesh and Tejaswi. The extreme subjectivity that had invaded Kannada modernity came under attack. This resulted in an altered sensibility and a demand for new aesthetics, and writers turned away from an excessive obsession with the individual predicament and showed a much more active engagement with societal issues. In other words, it was a great turning point in Kannada writing as it moved from an acute sense of the 'private' to a more nuanced 'public' domain.

D'Souza did not identify himself with any of these literary movements, though his writing career began in the mid-1960s and continued during the subsequent decades. But it would be wrong to say that he was a complete outsider and was untouched by their influence. He wrote at a time when Navya and later Bandaya movements were at their peak, but he did not declare his affiliation to any particular movement like many of his contemporaries did. That he was not at the forefront of any of these movements does not mean he was oblivious to their presence. At the same time, it needs to be noted that his writings do not overtly exhibit any sustained engagement with the main currents of Kannada literary movements. It is perhaps for this reason that Kannada mainstream criticism, obsessed as it is with a sense of aesthetic excellence and a tendency to view anything 'popular' with scepticism, has not paid serious attention to his writings. And D'Souza is not alone in this treatment, a point that has also been noted by some critics.

Given his active interest and participation, even to this day, in various social movements, particularly related to environmental issues, in and around Sagar town where he lives, it would be unfair to describe him as a mute spectator confined to the margins. Perhaps he felt there was no need to be a part of any particular literary movement to write what he felt passionately about. His strength as a writer seems to stem from his ability to remain open to the ideas generated by movements as well as maintain a critical distance from them. This is not to suggest, as some critics are fond of suggesting, that as a writer he stands 'above all ideologies'. On the contrary, it may well be the case that he can observe life from close quarters without being swayed by any one particular dominating point of view. This quality, coupled with his simple narrative style, will perhaps explain his popularity as a writer. His wide range of creative output – he is one of the most prolific writers in Kannada with nearly a hundred works to his credit – stands testimony to the fact that he has a larger number of readers than many of his contemporaries.

Having worked in the Sharavathi River Valley project, he had witnessed the entire activity of dam building from beginning to end, and had observed the apathy of bureaucracy. He had first-hand experience of studying the project's effects on the lives of poor and marginalized village folk. Moreover, he had moved closely among people living in interior forests, not as a part of his work, but as his own calling.

Viewed in this context, it is not surprising that many of his novels and short stories deal with the issue of submergence leading to displacement and provide an insider's view of the great sustaining force that enables the poor to face both natural and man-made adversities with great dignity and poise despite tragic consequences. Apart from several short stories, three of his novels, *Dweepa* (Island, 1978), *Mulugade* (Submersion, 1984), and *Oddu* (Dam/Barricade, 1990), deal with the tragedy of families being displaced due to highly insensitive and destructive 'development' projects. Each of them throws light on different aspects of this modern tragedy. While *Dweepa* portrays the agony caused by the rising backwater, leading to separation of human lives and hearts, *Oddu* depicts the heartlessness of bureaucracy which refuses to provide compensation for families whose lands are above the full reservoir level, but nevertheless marooned by the backwater. Absurd as it may sound, these are real stories and there are people still fighting for justice in many parts of Karnataka. It is the uncertainty of survival that finally leads to the tragic end. *Mulugade*, on the other hand, provides a picture of how people negotiate their destinies differently once they leave their ancestral homes and start their lives afresh. While very few manage to make their lives better, others do not and some even find in it an opportunity to exploit the situation at the cost of hapless victims of displacement. The three novels can be read as a trilogy, and together they offer a kaleidoscopic depiction of the complexities of human life, the avoidable loss of certain forms of living and belief systems, and the inevitability of negotiating new modes of being. The turbulence within the serene-looking, placid backwater is barely visible, but D'Souza dives deep and brings into view the tragedy of separated hearts, their unfulfilled dreams, and the loss of a way of life itself.

Dweepa brings a close-up view of life in a remote hamlet facing submergence and provides an insider's view of what it means to live amidst the fear of being marooned. Rendered in his usual style of simple and straight narration, the novella unfolds the tragedy that awaits the only family left behind, struggling to put its life together in a remote area that is soon going to be an island. Though there are several novels in Kannada with nature functioning as a living presence in the backdrop, in very few of them does nature become a character, driving the plot of the novel to its final destiny. *Dweepa* is one such work where the river Sharavathi, now bound by a dam, frames the narrative and remains in the foreground till the novel reaches its denouement. It reflects the changing mood of the protagonists, sometimes threatening and at other times protective. The river's eternal companion, rain, also plays a significant role. The chapters are named after the stars that influence the different phases of the monsoon, each suggesting a different mood and behaviour of the rains corresponding to the changes that happen in quick succession in the lives of the three individuals that inhabit the novella. Thus, nature, both as an external presence and an internal force, shapes the structure of the novella, pushing it to its final resolution.

At the very beginning we are told that the three families that came to inhabit the small patch of land at the foot of Sita Parvatha, a small hillock, had to struggle against nature to establish their settlements. There is a suggestion that this is a sort of benevolent intervention that nature tolerates and even nurtures the labouring human beings to enjoy the fruits of their work. Their status depended not so much on how much land they owned but on the fact that they did have some cultivable land. In fact, the novella opens with this remark:

> Ganapayya was neither rich nor poor. All he had were two acres of wetland for arecanut and three acres of agricultural land to grow rice. He did not own any farm hands; he hired some for wages. But that did not make any difference to his status. The respect the landlords commanded came from their place and role in the community, not from their wealth. This had been the system in the Malenadu villages for generations.

Ganapayya's family may not be as rich or as comfortably placed as the other two, but there is a suggestion that they lived as equals and even depended on one another, despite the difference in their economic status. But once Ganapayya learns that he is not going to receive the compensation as easily as others had received theirs, doubts begin to crop up. Ganapayya not only feels left out, but also feels he has been discriminated against. This makes him feel inferior to others and fills him with rage and even self-doubt. This is the first sign of the dam causing an unspoken rift, a small hiatus in the natural bonding that existed earlier. This sense of inferiority affects his relations with his wife, Nagaveni, and reaches a crescendo after the arrival of Krishnayya. There is a suggestion in the novella that the fissures that develop in the couple's relationship may not entirely be of their own making. There is an external force in the form of the dam that slowly inundates the village as well as the complex web of relationships that had sustained them at other adverse times.

> 'I can't eat a wholesome meal. I can't sleep to forget my troubles. I can't speak with my heart open. I can't trust anyone as my own, hug anyone as mine,' thought Krishnayya, 'the householder, Ganapayya might be feeling the same way. Nagaveni too. Each of us is shackled to a log but we can't sit still; we have to carry it on our heads and carry on with whatever needs to be done. Added to that, I feel there's a thorn in my heel festering, hurting at every step…. Ayyo, What a life!'

The dam becomes a symbol of man-made evil that threatens not just livelihoods but also human relations. The obstruction to the river is violence committed on Nature and hence is bound to result in counter-violence. While it submerges long-held belief-systems and values, it also brings to the fore the hidden evil, lurking in the form of a tiger that starts invading human habitation since its habitat too is disturbed. Nature, otherwise benevolent, can also reciprocate with fury when disturbed by damming. The symbolic significance of the rising water, engulfing the mythical hillock, is too hard to miss. The overbearing physical reality that surrounds and threatens their lives thus functions as a trope suggestive of their inner turmoil. *Dweepa* is as much a state of mind as it is of the outside nature.

There is also a hint in the novella that all is not over and there is a way out, if only the characters seek to know it. There is nothing inevitable about their predicament. Even though the novella moves towards a predictable ending, the tragedy that strikes them becomes poignant because it is avoidable. Look at how Krishnayya views his own condition:

> Krishnayya would have gone home if only the water around Hosamane had subsided, if only there were no wild animals on the prowl around the house. He stayed on mainly for Nagaveni's sake, for whatever pleasure she got out of his presence.

Since the time *Dweepa* was first published, displacements caused by developmental projects have taken a new turn and have risen to alarming proportions. In fact, the term 'displacement' holds the key to understanding the essential crisis of our times. It is often said that while modern India basks in the glory of its development, Bharat pays for this progress in the form of starving and struggling people. As a fictional work *Dweepa* may not capture all the complexities of development-induced disasters and the growing gap between India and Bharat that we are facing today. The simplicity of narration and the lack of density of detail that gives life force to a work of art may have prevented the novella from realizing its fiction potential. But ironically, what the novella lacks is provided by the growing complexity of our times that fills it with new meaning.

Dweepa certainly holds the unseen and untold Bharat in its womb.

V.S. Sreedhara

Kinship Terms

amma   mother
appayya   father (appa = father, ayya = a term/
                      suffix denoting respect)
athige   sister-in-law
ayya   familiar term of address between
                      equals, also maharaya/maaraaya
bava/bavayya   brother-in-law
koosu   child; koose – form of addressing a
                      child
maga   son
maani   boy
mava   father-in-law
odeya   master
sose   daughter-in-law

thatha   grandfather; familiar way of address-
                      ing an elderly person
yajamanaru   master

Krithika

Ganapayya
was neither rich nor poor. All he had were two acres of
wetland for an areca farm and three acres of agricultural
land to grow rice. He did not own farm hands; he hired
some for wages. But that did not make any difference to
his status. The respect the landlords commanded came
from their place and role in the community, not from
their wealth. This had been the system in the Malenadu
villages for generations.

When Ganapayya crossed the bridge from the
farm, came down the valley, and turned towards his
house, he saw the Sharavathi. An ominous bit of news
about the river had been ringing in his ears. An elderly
peon who had come from the Submersion Office in
Kargal to see Herambha Hegde had met him with,

'Sharavathi might swallow the Hosamane Parvatha this monsoon'.

But the same man had prophesied the same doom the previous year. The Linganamakki Dam had not even risen ten feet then. The surveyors had said that the dam would not fill up. And yet, Ganapayya, Herambha Hegde, and Parameshwarayya were worried. They had hastened to the Submersion Office to check if there was any truth in what the peon had said.

'Nothing of that sort will happen,' the government officials had snapped. 'You can stay on peacefully until we compensate you with land elsewhere.'

And so they had lived without anxiety for another year. The water in the Sharavathi did not rise; the Hosamane village was not submerged. As usual, they had grown arecanut on the farms and rice in the paddy fields. And had reaped a good harvest, sold their produce, and had lived happily.

But now the dam had grown like a huge wall. They were told that water would surely collect in it this year. Would it submerge Hosamanehalli as the old man predicted?

'If that should happen, what will happen to my house?' Ganapayya feared.

Ganapayya stopped in the valley, staring at the river. The Sharavathi was just about a shout away from the row of houses. During summer she hardly held any water. But during the monsoon she was on the verge of overflowing. Even then, the water that overran the banks barely touched the paddy fields. That was about all. There was no danger to the fields or the farms. Now that the dam was being built across the river, the water level could surely rise higher. The government officials had installed a red stone on the forehead of Sita Parvatha behind the village to show how high the water would rise once the dam was ready. But the old man had insisted that the village would be inundated that very year.

'Why this year? Let it drown right now,' groaned Ganapayya in despair. 'The government has set out to ruin thousands of homes. Is it a big deal for it to drown my village, my home? But what about the compensation they say they'll give us? When will *that* come?

'All kinds of filthy strangers have stomped on our lands, measuring the fields, the farms, the house, the byre, the outhouse, the garden. They've set a price on everything. They've asked, "Where would you like us to give you land?" But that was over a year ago. Since then, there's been a monsoon, a winter, and a summer. And now the rain clouds are thundering for another monsoon. Of the five houses in the village, two belong to bonded labourers. They get no compensation, anyway, for they have nothing to call their own. The remaining three families will be duly compensated, they said.

'That Parameshwarayya may have gone to the office and greased their palms; he got his compensation pretty quickly. They've given him lands near Sagara. Herambha too might have done something of that sort. There's news that he'll be compensated very soon. But what about me? That surveyor Shetty at the Submersion Office says my file is missing, lost. I've been there over ten times now. And every time it's the same old story. And as if that's not bad enough, this old man is scaring me now. I must go again tomorrow.'

Ganapayya walked towards his house.

To one side of the village Hosamanehalli flowed the Sharavathi, on the other was Sita Parvatha. It was named after Sree Rama's wife but it was no mountain despite its name. It was neither that tall nor that wide; it was a mere hillock. Its back was lush with forestlands but its head was bald. Sree Rama, Sita, and Lakshmana were said to have come there when they were banished from Ayodhya. They had crossed the Sharavathi and had rested for a few days in a cave formed by some huge boulders near the crest of the hill. Right inside the grotto was a granite slab shaped like a cot by wind and rain. This was known as Sita-Rama's bed.

Sprawled at the foot of the hill were five families, three areca plantations, and three rice fields. Of the five families, three were those of the landlords who owned the areca farms and the paddy fields, the other two were of the bonded labourers, bonded since birth because their fathers had not been able to pay off their debts to the landlords. Of the three landlords, Herambha Hegde and Parameshwarayya were wealthy; they owned the bonded labourers of the Hasalaru community, Byra and Hala, who worked on their land.

Beyond the Sharavathi, towards the east, were towns like Talaguppa, Hiremane, and Sagara. To the west were places like Aralagodu and Bheemeshwara. The people of Hosamanehalli had contact only with the towns in the east because it was easy to cross the river during summer. The river bed was wide and strewn with huge boulders. Jumping from one to another to another, they could get to the other bank. But they could never do that during the monsoon when the Sharavathi was brimming and gushing, when not a boulder could be seen, when the water was thick and murky. No one needed to cross the river during the monsoon anyway. Even as the rainy season neared, a stock of groceries and other such commodities came from Talaguppa-Sagara, enough to last for four months. If there was still any need to go to Sagara, there was always the Thumri-Byakodi road.

These people had lived in this way for over fifty years. The coconut and jackfruit trees in front of Herambha Hegde's house spoke of the antiquity of Hosamanehalli. His house was the oldest in the village. When Herambha's grandfather left a place near Mavinagundi and bought a piece of land, built a house, and settled down here, his place came to be called Hosamane, the new house. Herambha's house became old but the village retained the name – Hosamanehalli – the village of the new house.

Now the time had come for the village to drown. Sharavathi had never come close to Hosamanehalli though she would roar ferociously from a distance during the monsoon. But she was now thinking of swallowing it up. These days her water did not flow freely; it stagnated in deep pools, waiting dangerously.

This was what Ganapayya noticed as he walked towards the house from the farm. If the flooded river gushed away in a torrent, there was always the relief of surviving a great peril. But what would happen if the flood was stalled? Or what would happen if the deluge flowed continuously? The warnings of the old man from the Submersion Office echoed in Ganapayya's ears.

The Sharavathi lay only to one side of Hosamanehalli, no doubt. But with the Linganamakki Dam coming up, it was quite possible she would overflow from all sides.

Then she could branch out on either side of the Sita Parvatha and reunite to flow on. Not just that. As the water-level rose, it would not be impossible for her to gulp down the hillock she encircled bit by bit until she swallowed it completely, once and for all. If Sita Parvatha could drown, what chance of survival did Hosamanehalli or Ganapayya-Herambha-Parameshwarayya's houses-fields-farms have? If the houses of the landlords could get submerged, what would be the plight of the labourers' hutments?

That was the reason the government had announced compensation for the displaced families; a payment at a fixed rate for farm hand, agricultural land, house, well, cowshed.... Some were also given land elsewhere. The government had provided transport to the families to move their bags and baggage to the new places. It had also sent notices to the landlords, asking them to move out before a specified date. Parameshwarayya was so unnerved on receiving the notice that he left the village almost immediately. With him went his bonded labourer, Hala, and his family.

Now there were only three houses left in Hosamanehalli: Herambha's, his farm hand Byra's, and Ganapayya's. There was a rumour that compensation had been sanctioned for Herambha. He had planted rice seedlings, hoping to stay on. But if he did get his money and was asked to move, he would have to move. And if Herambha went, Byra, his bonded labourer, would go with him. And then there would be only one house in the village – Ganapayya's!

Ganapayya strode towards his house as if he was entering a forest where a tiger lurked. Duggajja lay on a bed on a platform to one side of the veranda. He coughed and groaned on seeing his son.

'Ganapa, did Herambha meet you?'

'No, I'm coming from the farm. Why, Appayya? Did he come here?'

'Yes. He said he wanted to see you.... It looks as if he's planning to leave this year.'

'Really?'

Ganapayya had come home gripped with the fear of a lurking tiger.... Where was it hiding? In the shade of which tree? Behind which boulder? He had come home fearing from where would it spring on him and now it had sprung on him from behind. He slipped his feet back into the slippers he had just taken off and walked out again. His wife, who had been standing by the door, went indoors.

Herambha had told him they should spend the year together. He had asked for land near Ananthapura. But he had decided to stay on through the monsoon and move to the new place after the rainy season. So what had happened now for him to want to move all of a sudden? Ganapayya wiped the sweat off his face with the towel on his shoulder and walked down the valley towards Herambha's farm.

There was great commotion at the farm. People were pulling down the thatched roofing of the farmhouse. The house too was in a bustle. The cowshed was being dismantled; long wooden roofing beams were pulled down and stacked. Labourers from the Deevru community from Aralagodu were busy on the job. So it was certain that Herambha was leaving.

But why?

Seeing Ganapayya climbing up the steps to the garden, Herambha came forward.

'Ganapayya, I had been to your house. Did your father tell you?'

'Yes, he did. I just returned from the farm. I came as soon as I heard you'd come to see me. But why all this?'

'This is the reason I came to you, to tell you about this. Come here, let's sit down.'

As Ganapayya followed Herambha on to the veranda and sat on a mat with him, Herambha looked towards the door and said to his daughter, 'Koose, Ganapayya's come', but loud enough for his wife to hear him.

'My records have been finalized at the Submersion Office, Ganapayya,' he said, 'I myself saw the papers.

The farm, field, and house are valued at fifty thousand rupees for now and the money has been sanctioned. The Ananthapura land too is in my name. They have also provided money for me to clear forestland for cultivation … I'll have to move from here today or tomorrow, anyway. Why should I stay on and strain myself through the monsoon, craving to reap a profit from harvesting areca nut and paddy? Who knows how high the water will rise this year? The hillock may not drown. But where's the guarantee that our lands won't? That's why I've decided to move. The government lorries are coming tomorrow to transport everything.'

Herambha's daughter brought a tumbler of coffee and placed it near him.

'Have this,' said Herambha.

Ganapayya lifted it to his lips mechanically. He did not know what to say about Herambha's decision. He clenched his teeth as if he had been flogged.

'Herambha … your job's done. Where will I go? What'll I do? I've decided not to move from here until I get the compensation and land due to me. It doesn't matter if the water rises and the village drowns and all of us die … I'll *never* move.'

'Go to the office once again, Ganapayya. They'll speed up work on your file if you bribe them some five or ten rupees.'

'I've given them, Herambha. I've given more than a hundred. All that's left is my life.'

Ganapayya took the towel off his shoulder, whacked it in disgust, and threw it on his shoulder again.

'I'll go, Herambha,' he said as he stood up and walked away briskly.

'This is just as I had feared. Once Herambha and Byra leave the place there would be just the three of us, Appayya, Nagaveni, and I. As the Sharavathi keeps rising encroaching the land around the village, the three of us will have to survive on this island for four months. We'll have no contact whatsoever with the world outside until the monsoon is over. How can we live here in this condition? I may say, enough of this problem, let's go elsewhere. But where can we go? I've depended on this farm and the field till now, where else can I live?'

'Maani, what did Herambha say?' his father asked anxiously as Ganapayya reached home.

'He's leaving, Appayya. The government has given him lands. It has sanctioned money too. He says he'll go to the new land and start cultivating it.... They were dismantling the byre.... Anyway, it's certain that he'll move with his family tomorrow or the day after.'

'Really?'

Duggajja sat staring at the areca palms swaying gently in the breeze.

'Maani, will the water come all over here this monsoon?'

'Whatever may happen, we're not moving out of here, Appayya. That's for sure.'

The old man sighed to see his son kicking the floor as he went inside the house.

And yet, this was what Duggajja had hoped for deep inside; that they would stay on at least for this year. Every time there was talk of having to leave Hosamanehalli, he felt weak in the legs and sank to the floor. He loved his piece of land with the attachment a woman feels for her mother's house. He was determined he would not leave her if he could help it. He had wondered a hundred times whether there was any way of carrying on here even when the village was covered with water. He had wished a thousand times that the dam would collapse. He had stopped every official who came on behalf of the government and had asked, 'Will Sita Parvatha really drown?' Most of them said whatever they felt the old man would like to hear from them. But some of them told him the truth; that water would stand at ten feet above the hillock. They also told him the dam would have to be built before it could hold that much of water. Some others had said there was no immediate danger to Hosamanehalli; it would take three years to complete the project.

'Why can't we stay on until then?' was Duggajja's stand, 'Where's the hurry to apply for compensation and ask for land elsewhere right now? Let it come in its own time. Anyway, we have enough to eat, don't we? Yes, water may cover the village. And yes, we may not get labourers to help on the land. But with the first rain, if we see to the planting and other such work on the farm and the field, we'll have to worry about harvesting only after the monsoon. We can always get someone to see to the odd jobs between planting and harvesting.'

That was how the old man felt but would his son feel the same way?

Ganapayya cursed the Submersion Office. He ranted as if he would go the very next day and pull down the place.

'Let's not live here during the monsoon. Let's go to my father's house,' suggested Nagaveni.

'And then? Are we to return after four months to eat cow-dung?' he roared at her, rolling up his sleeves. 'Even if the government compensates me with land and money right now, I'm not the kind who'll up and go immediately. I'm going to stay here this monsoon and reap a harvest on my land. Let whatever happens, happen.'

Ganapayya was happy when his father came inside and supported his decision.

'If you're so tired of staying here, go to your father's house,' he growled at his wife.

Another trend of thought soothed his tortured spirit: 'Anyway, Herambha's leaving his lands. Why can't I harvest them with mine? He can't uproot his rice seedlings and areca palms; he can't take them with him. And he has no one here to watch over them. Let me ask him before he leaves. He's sure to say yes. I'll tell him I'll give him a part of the harvest as his share. This seems to be a good plan. If the officials do come and bother me to leave, I can always bribe them a bit. Let's see.'

'Is the water hot for my bath, Naagu?' he asked his wife. There was spirit in his voice.

'Hmm,' replied Nagaveni. Her face was grumpy, like a shrivelled brinjal.

Ganapayya went up the attic, pulled down a pani-panche hanging from the cross pole, and wrapped the short strip of cloth around his waist. Then he loosened the full-length panche he was wearing and adjusted the *maunji* round his waist over the strip to hold it in place. Scratching his arm, he went into the bathroom.

The water came in a drainpipe cut out from areca trunks, all the way from a spring on the brow of Sita Parvatha, into his bathroom. Ganapayya's ears were attuned to the soothing sound as the water fell into a tank, *dhapa-dhapa*. Nagaveni filled a cauldron with the water, stuck a log in the fireplace, and lit it. As she left a bowl of soap nut powder for his bath and went inside, Ganapayya poured hot water on himself and sighed in great relief, 'Haa!'

The water washed away all the stress he had endured until that moment.

***

Herambha Hegde was a peculiar man; he was not at all avaricious. Though he had previously planned to stay on throughout the rainy season and harvest his produce for the year, he was willing to leave everything and move on once the compensation was sanctioned. He felt there was no need to stick on to his old way of life. He liked the new place allotted to him near Ananthapura. He was attracted to the city and so he decided to loosen the bonds that bound him to Hosamanehalli. Who knew what tomorrow would bring? He had a houseful of children, his wife was pregnant again. What if he needed help when the Sharavathi surrounded the village? What if they were marooned? What if the engineers had miscalculated and the village drowned that very monsoon? They had stayed there long enough. It was time to move on....

Herambha was ready to leave. The government lorries were packed with all his belongings, even the wooden beams, tiles, hay for thatched roof, everything.

'Herambha ...,' said Ganapayya.

'Aa, Ganapayya, I myself wanted to talk to you about that,' replied Herambha. 'Since you're going to stay on, you can harvest my fields and farm. After all, it's not as if they're *mine*. I just happened to own them, that's all. You don't have to give me a single areca nut. I've planted the rice saplings, yes. Whether you feel like giving me a share or not, it is up to you. You know why I say this? Because you'll have to work a lot more on the paddy field than I did before you can harvest it.'

And after a pause, Herambha said, 'Ganapayya, now there're only the three of you. Your father can hardly work. How much can you and your wife do? Get some farm hands from the Deevru community.'

Ganapayya nodded, 'What you say makes sense, Herambha. I'll need one or two of them for moral support besides help on the farm. Let me see if I can get some from Aralagodu or Hiremane.'

Herambha, his wife and children, Byra, his wife and children, finally bid farewell to Hosamanehalli and left. The two lorries that had been shunting back and forth for the past three days, wended their way towards the Talaguppa highway for the last time through the make-shift road beside the Sharavathi.

Ganapayya, Duggajja, and Nagamani felt depressed to see the lorries receding. They were filled with a vague dread too as if the isolation was ominous. They felt a sudden urge to up and go. But these feelings were temporary. Ganapayya slung his axe over his shoulder and set out to chop firewood to be stocked for the monsoon. As Belli ambled towards the cowshed, Nagaveni ran in to prevent the cow from feeding all her milk to her calf. The old man kept watch over the *happala* drying in the sun lest crows should get at them. The air that came to them over the Sharavathi was cool and comforting. So were the wispy white clouds.

***

Ganapayya went to the Submersion Office in Kargal.

'Oho, how is it that you've come this far, Swami?' said the old peon sitting at the door of the officer's chamber, displaying all his rotten teeth. Ganapayya pushed him aside and barged into the room.

'Both Parameshwarayya and Herambha Hegde have received compensation for their property in Hosamanehalli. What sin have I committed that I shouldn't get mine, Swami?' he asked the officer, 'Do you wish that my father, my wife, and I should meet our death by water this monsoon?'

The officer was a mild-mannered person, a very patient man. He understood the brusque ways of villagers like Ganapayya.

'Please sit down,' he said. Ganapayya sat on a stool. He felt he should not have shouted so rudely. And so he started all over again and presented his petition courteously. The officer pressed the bell on his table and asked the peon to call the person concerned.

The surveyor who had been to Hosamanehalli came in and stood in front of him trembling with fear.

'What is this, Shetty? This person says his case has not been settled yet. Why?'

'It's settled, Saar. The cheque is ready.' Shetty looked shifty, uncomfortable.

'What do you mean by "it's settled"? Have you given land and other compensations to all the families in Hosamanehalli?'

The officer could make out the truth from the way Shetty was avoiding his piercing stare.

'Parameshwarayya and Herambha Hegde have received theirs, Saar.'

'What about this person?'

'No, Saar.' Shetty began to perspire.

'Why? He didn't bribe you enough, perhaps, the poor man.'

The officer had rapped him gently but Shetty felt he had been slapped with a slipper at the crossroads. He stood with his head bowed.

'What happened to his case, Shetty?'

'His ... his file is ... missing ... lost, Sir.'

'Oho, so that's how it is, is it?'

The officer looked at Ganapayya. He felt bad. He could not bear to see the farmers suffer in so many new unreasonable ways for no sin of theirs.

'Look here, mister. I'll take the responsibility of settling your dues as soon as the monsoon is over. Don't get frightened. Even if Hosamanehalli is marooned, the water will subside after the rains. You go home now.'

He spoke so gently that Ganapayya could do nothing but leave the place. As he crossed the threshold he could hear the officer taking Shetty to task. He felt relieved.

Ganapayya caught a bus to Aralagodu and from there took a bylane to Hosamane. It was certain now that his connection to his village had not yet been severed.

'Let's see what happens', he said to himself as he trod the familiar pathway. In the distance he could see dark clouds massing over the brow of Sita Parvatha.

Rohini

On this bank of the Sharavathi was the row of Hosamane fields. They were sprawled all over the sloping back of Sita Parvatha. Parameshwarayya's lands in the distance looked uncared for; unkempt with weeds and shrubs.

It was six months since his areca farm had been razed to the ground. Some minister was visiting some place in Sagara and so all the areca palms on his land were chopped off and taken away to decorate the place.

Tender green finger-long seedlings of paddy were standing in Ganapayya's fields. So also in Herambha's. Right in the middle was Ganapayya's house and beyond the fields was Herambha's extensive areca farm. And beyond that, as far as the eye could see, was what used to be Parameshwarayya's areca farm, once flourishing, now desolate. To one side of the areca farms had stood the houses of the labourers, Byra and Hala before they were dismantled and taken away.

Now there was only one house standing, Ganapayya's, the only house in Hosamanehalli.

When Ganapayya was on his way back home after seeing to a few jobs on the farm, he saw Nagaveni walking towards the farm. By the time he washed his hands and feet in the pond and came towards the bund, she was close enough....

'You know, Belli hasn't come home at all.'

Nagaveni always addressed him as 'you know'. The expression signalled that she was talking to him.

'Really?' Ganapayya asked her in the same anxious tone of voice she had used.

A shy blush mingled with the tension on her face.

'Shee ... Is this any time to joke?'

The evening sun had spread lazily over the fields, making the greenery a translucent yellow. Nagaveni too looked delicate as if sprouting tender green leaves like everything else around them. Ganapayya caught his breath with the tightness of hunger, of desire. He stood transfixed.

'You know, did you hear me? Belli hasn't come home yet.'

'I heard you. That's why I said "Really?" didn't I?'

'Yes, she hasn't come home yet,' repeated Nagaveni lamely.

'The bull from the Gowda's cart had come this way while he was collecting sand from the river bed. She might've gone after him.'

'Sheee ...!' said Nagaveni.

Ganapayya cast a glance all over the farm. It was quite some time since the farm hands from Aralagodu had left. There was no one around. Father was not the sort to stir out of the house. And, anyway, why would anyone else come this far?

As Nagaveni looked lost, looking around for Belli, Ganapayya darted towards her and grabbed her.

'Ayyo, let go, let go of me!' she cried, struggling to break free but he hugged her tender body to his own, kissed her cheek and groaned, 'Naaguu!'

Nagaveni slipped out of his embrace and ran ahead of him.

'What is this child's play?' she said as she came out of the farm. Ganapayya followed her.

'She may be grazing on the hill,' he said, 'I'll look for Belli and bring her. You go on – go home.'

But Nagaveni did not go home. 'Come, let's go. I'll come along with you,' she said instead.

The two of them climbed the hillock.

This was the fourth time they had walked up Sita Parvatha together. Soon after they had got married, Ganapayya had taken Nagaveni right up to the cavern and had shown her Sita-Rama's bed. The second time was when Krishnayya had come. And the third time was when Belli had calved in the cave. In the three years since Nagaveni had entered his life, this was the fourth time they were climbing the Parvatha that lay behind their house.

Ganapayya did not often go right up to the crest of the hill. There was no need to. He could get all the firewood they needed from the trees on the slope. If he had to go that far, it had to be under unusual circumstances, like this one when cows or calves strayed away. But even then, he did not always have to go all the way to the top. Quite often such stray cattle could be found in the meadows below or in the jungles of Aralagodu. Very rarely did they go that far. Only Belli was used to climbing all the way up. She had calved in the cave once. Could she have gone up there again?

Ganapayya walked up a winding path on the back of the mountain. Nagaveni followed him, calling out, 'Belli! Belli!' from time to time. He turned back and laughed at her strangely.

'What's so funny, you know?' she asked.

'Woman, I told you I'd look for Belli, didn't I? Why are you coming after me like the tail behind a bull?'

'A bull or a bison. Do I have to teach you to talk? It's been a long time since I've been up the Parvatha. That's why I'm coming with you.'

'Okay, come. But if there's a tiger up there, don't expect me to protect you.'

'Oho, a tiger, is it? You're a big tiger yourself. Can there be another?'

As she giggled tantalizingly, Ganapayya stretched out his hand towards her. She leaned towards him and the two of them walked briskly together in the enveloping twilight.

The view from Sita Parvatha was clear; they could see some three to four miles all around. The Sharavathi had spread out quite a bit to one side. The Linganamakki Dam stood as if it held three or four hills in its embrace. Nestling against the dam was a huge expanse of water lying like the sea amidst forests and ravines. One edge of this body of water had stretched itself right against the foot of the hillock on which they were standing. Beyond the other edge was forestland on low-lying hills and beyond that, in the distance, was a faint glimmer of light. To a side rose a spiral of smoke; from a forest fire, perhaps. The horizon was a trail of reddish streaks against grey skies, left behind by the setting sun.

When Nagaveni went into the cave, calling out to Belli and stretched herself on Sita-Rama's bed, Ganapayya too lay down beside her and kissed her lips. Belli, who had been grazing somewhere behind the cavern, heard her mistress through the boulders, came and stood at the entrance and responded, '*ambaa*'. Ganapayya was aware of her only when she called the second time. He disentangled himself from Nagaveni's embrace, sat up, and threw a stone at her shouting, '*Thu*! You harlot of a cow! Go home!'

And Belli promptly turned homewards.

Nagaveni's rigid body slackened slowly. She rearranged her pallu over her shoulder and sat up, trying to still her heaving breath. The forest fire had burnt itself out, leaving a dull bluish haze in the distance. The open mouth of the empty cave looked grotesque as she left the still warm Sita-Rama's bed and walked over to her husband who stood outside with his back to the cave. As they walked back in silence a wild fowl set up a continuous raucous call.

***

Duggajja sat on the parapet just beyond the thatched awning. The farm hands who had completed the day's work came to him, asking, 'Odeya, can we go home now?' And they had gone back to Aralagodu.

'The *sose* went towards the farm quite some time ago grumbling that Belli hadn't come home. And there's no sign of her since then. Could my *maga* and sose have gone together looking for Belli? Can't they come back soon? It's getting dark. Where could they've gone?' the old man wondered.

He tried to walk a few steps leaning on his stick but felt unsteady. It seemed an effort to lift each foot and put it forward. He went back to the entrance and sat reminiscing. There was a time when he could walk all over Hosamanehalli not once but a thousand times. He was just a stripling when his father had started to farm the land but he could work with his parents shoulder to shoulder. He had sown areca and banana saplings, weeded the land, tied areca sheaths around the fronds to protect the nuts and then he had climbed trees, cut down nuts, peeled them, and stored them in neat piles. His father used to put his arm over his shoulders and say, 'Having this one boy to work with me is like having a hundred farm hands.'

Even in those days, there were not many houses in Hosamanehalli, only four – Herambha Hegde's, his labourer, Byra's, Parameshwarayya's, and his own. Parameshwarayya had not yet become wealthy enough to own a bonded labourer. All these men were still young, barely eight or ten years older than Ganapayya. His father and Herambha's father, Subbaraya, were the only elders in those days. His father died early. Subbaraya lived to a ripe old age; right until people started saying among themselves, 'This old man has no death'. He had died recently. He could easily have been a hundred years when he died.

Duggajja wondered how old he himself was. Sixty, perhaps. But he felt like an old man, wasting away with illness. Now that his son had got him some medicine from Sagara for his cough and wheezing, he was a little better than he used to be. But whenever the rains came he was confined to bed. It was ten to fifteen years since he had started this dreadful wheezing. He had tried every herbal concoction but nothing had helped.

The old man sat still. A cool breeze wafted in from the farm. The hillock behind the house and farm cast a deep shadow on them. The birds had stopped chirping. A few clouds were drifting in the darkening sky. Only the water from the pond in the farm was flowing lazily. The old man looked all around him. As he saw Herambha's farm and the walls of his dismantled house, fear clutched at his heart.

'What a fate for an innocent village!' the old man grieved, 'Just four to five families; a few people with their joys and pain. We had everything here. But now, all we have is barrenness. It wasn't as if this village had people spilling over, bustling with excitement as on the main street in Talaguppa town. It was always like this, quiet and restful with hardly any people about. But there was the security of neighbourliness, a feeling that if I called out to Herambha or Prameshwarayya, one or the other would come; a certainty that Byra and Hala were somewhere around the place.

'Now, who can I call? If I shout "Coo", will it reach Aralagodu or Bheemeshwara? Will those people heed my call and come all this way? And if things are so bad now, how will it be once the rains come and this place is covered with water? We may not even get labourers to work on the farm and the field. How much can my family do? I must tell Ganapa to see if we can get some men here before the monsoon. We've decided to stay on for this year for better, for worse, whether it's wise or not. But there's always the fear of what might happen after that.'

Belli came ambling down the hill and made her way towards the back of the house.

'The cow is home…. Where did these two go?'

As the old man peered into the distance, he saw his son emerging from the darkness. And behind him was the daughter-in-law.

'Koose, Belli's gone to the backyard,' the old man called out to her. She did not respond but rushed into the house.

Ganapayya sat beside his father and told him how Belli had gone right up the hillock, how he and his wife had gone there looking for her and had brought her back. It was pitch dark by the time he finished his story. Nagaveni lit a lamp and placed it on the platform.

During dinner they talked of getting some farm hands to stay with them throughout the monsoon. Herambha had suggested that Ganapayya should get a few Nayak men from the Deevru community as the regular daily-wage labourers from Aralagodu were not willing to stay on the land. They resented the extra work, of course, but they were also afraid of what might happen to the village during the rains. They would have to look after Herambha's field and farm besides Ganappaya's. Once water surrounded the hillock they would probably not be able to get extra labour. Ganapayya might get one or two men for the season. But planting rice seedlings and sheathing the arecanut fronds would need more than three or four people even if Ganapayya and his wife joined them. That was why the men from Aralagodu had refused to stay.

'Right now, we could do with a man and a woman', said Duggajja, 'and later on we could get a few more, can't we?'

'Why shouldn't we bring a Deevru or a Hasalaru family?' thought Ganapayya. 'If we provide them with house, food, and clothes, they might stay the five months. They can go back when we move on.' And turning to his father, he said, 'I'll go to Talaguppa tomorrow. Let's see.'

After the old man finished his dinner and went outside, Nagaveni asked her husband while serving him, 'You know, are you going to Talaguppa tomorrow?'

'Yes. Why?'

'I was just wondering ... It's so long since I've seen Amma.... Once the rains come we won't be able to stir out of the house....'

Nagaveni's mother's house was quite close to Talaguppa. She had been there last during the Bellaane temple fair. And she had never visited her family again. They had sent word asking her to go over but how could she unless her husband sent her?

'Appayya will be alone in the house ...'

Yes, that was a problem. Was it wise to leave an ailing old man alone and go? Nagaveni stared at her husband's face to see if he would think of a way out.

'Let's take the ten o'clock Gajanana bus and return as quickly as possible. Appayya may not mind staying alone for those few hours.'

Nagaveni nodded happily.

Previously, the distance from Hosamanehalli to Talaguppa was a mere six miles, from Hosamane to Hiremane and thence to Talaguppa. All they had to do was cross the Sharavathi. But now it was twenty miles. Since the old road was submerged, they had to get to Aralagodu, go to Kargal from there, and then to Talaguppa. Where they used to pay eight annas previously, they now paid a rupee and eight. Where they once took half an hour to cover the distance, they now took an hour and a half.

Dugajja was quite willing to send his son and daughter-in-law off on a mission to get farm hands who would stay with them through the monsoon. They told the daily-wage labourers to sheath the arecanuts, had an early lunch, and set off.

'Get red chillies, dhall, and other such groceries. Anyway, the monsoon will be here,' Dugajja reminded his son.

'Yes, I will,' replied Ganapayya as he walked away with his wife.

'Will the water come all this way?' Nagaveni asked her husband as they set their backs to the hillock and walked on. They took the road from Hosamane to Aralagodu. Though it was on an elevation, the government officials had planted red stones all the way to show how high the water would reach when the dam was done.

'Not this year, perhaps', Ganapayya replied, adding, 'if it doesn't rise this high we shouldn't have any problems. People will still be able to come here and we'll be able to go out. But how can we be absolutely sure it won't? What guarantee is there in what the government says? Anyway, if the water does rise, we'll be in trouble. We'll be stranded until it goes down again.'

Nagaveni was not unduly perturbed. She was happy with the thoughts of visiting her mother's house. There was a spring in her step and laughter in her voice. Her face was suffused with a glow which made her so attractive that Ganapayya felt a special tenderness towards her.

They crossed the bridge, walked past Aithumane, and reached Aralagodu in time for the bus. It was small, old, and rickety. The commuters were crammed like pickled lime but the conductor did not want to leave anyone behind. So Ganapayya and Nagaveni got in.

And the bus lumbered past place names etched on stone slabs – Kargal, Idavani, Bachagaru, Talavata, Hiremane.... People who had to get down got down and those who wanted to get in got in. By the time it reached Talaguppa, the sky was overcast and the wind fearsome. Ganapayya was looking for someone familiar with whom he could send Nagaveni to her mother's house when she called out to him, 'You know, isn't that Krishnayya?'

Krishnayya came running up to them with, 'Bava, how is it you're here? And how're you, Nagu?' he said.

'Nagu, come back here by five. I'll be waiting for you,' said Ganapayya.

Nagaveni nodded.

'Why don't you come with us, Bava?' asked Krishnayya.

'I've got to see to something else,' replied Ganapayya and walked away towards Bhatta's shop.

By the time Nagaveni and Krishnayya crossed the railway track and walked towards their house, the wind became gusty. There was a cloud-burst; lightning shattered the sky, bringing down a thunder shower. Krishnayya opened his umbrella and held it towards Nagaveni but she took a few moments to move under it. Even when she walked beside him, she held herself together in the heavy rain.

Krishnayya had grown up in Nagaveni's house. He was ten years older than her. Nagaveni's father had brought him to work in the house but had raised him like a member of the family. He was Krishnayya to Nagaveni. Her husband was Bava to Krishnayya, a brother-in-law.

Krishnayya was tall and fair, a strapping young man. Not just that. He had a luxuriant moustache on his broad face. He was friendly. Everyone in his neighbourhood was familiar with his winsome smile. And he had the zest to do the work of ten people.

Nagaveni was fond of him. She was always happy in his presence, whether listening to his stories or watching him at work. He too felt the same way towards her.

When Nagaveni got married and left for her husband's house, it was Krishnayya who had wept the most. People said he had not eaten for three days. He had gone right up to Talaguppa to see her off.

'Nagu, I'll go back now. You go on to your husband's house,' he had said. And she had wept her heart out. Only she knew she was crying for him. The others thought it was but natural for a bride to weep when she left her mother's house for the first time. Of course, she had also wept to go away to a strange house. But then, she needed a reason to cope with the ache in her heart, didn't she?

The rain became torrential and while Nagaveni was drenched on one side of the umbrella, Krishnayya was soaked on the other. Somehow they reached home under that one umbrella.

Nagaveni spent a few hours with her parents, brothers, and younger sister.

'Stay on,' said her mother as she was leaving.

'No, Amma. He wants us to get back this evening,' replied Nagaveni and bid everyone goodbye.

Krishnayya went along with her to the bus stand.

The thunderstorm had passed. The trees looked fresh and vibrant in the dull sunlight. The sky was washed clean and blue. Water stood everywhere in little puddles, glistening. The rice fields were green with shoots of paddy.

'Are you going far away, Nagu?'

'Not now. After the rains. They've given land and money to everyone else in our village. Everyone but us. We're the only family in Hosamane now.'

'Really?'

'Yes. That's why he's come to Talaguppa to look for labourers who'll stay and work the land with us throughout the rains.'

'Shall I come?'

'Come.'

'I can come right away. Feed me two meals a day and I'll do the work of ten people.'

Nagaveni looked up at him and laughed.

Ganapayya was waiting for them. Krishnayya helped in loading the bag of groceries on top of the bus. Nagaveni's face looked pinched as the bus moved. Krishnayya waved at them as they sped away.

'Were you able to get someone to stay with us?' Nagaveni asked her husband as they walked towards their village.

'No. It doesn't look as if we can get anyone. I asked everywhere, in Talaguppa, Manamane, and Marthuru. No one's willing to come.... Don't know what we should do.... It would've been good to have someone now that the rain's upon us. How can we live on our own here?'

Nagaveni walked silently, a little ahead of her husband.

'Perhaps our Krishnayya would come if we asked him,' she said, turning towards him.

'Krishnayya? Yes, maybe we could ask him. But who'll see to the work there, at your father's house?'

'There'll always be someone there. Deevru farm hands are easy to get in that place. Send word to Krishnayya tomorrow or the day after. Let him come.'

'Let's do that.'

It was dusk by the time they passed Aithumane and came to the bridge. It had rained heavily. There was water everywhere – a sure sign the monsoon had set in. The Rohini rains had been coming on and off the past four days. The saplings in the fields stood with their heads held high. The land that had shrivelled up in the sun was now wet and pliant. Some farmers had started to plough and sow. Heavy wind, thunder, and lightning were harbingers of the *mirugi* phase of the monsoon. Once this intermittent rain became incessant, it would stop only after four months. Ganapayya had to stock up everything they needed and chop more firewood. He had to repair the farmhouse; it needed a new thatch. There were quite a few things to be seen to.

'I'd better send for Krishnayya tomorrow,' he said to himself.

They could see the burning lamp on the platform.

'O, Appayya's got up and lit the lamp. Poor old man!' said Ganapayya.

Even as they neared the house, he heard his soft voice, 'Maani?'

'We're here,' he said as they stepped into the awning at the door.

Mrigashira

It was the feast of the Mirugi rain and so none of the farm hands had come to work that day. The first phase of work on the farm had been completed anyway. Only the thatch roof on the farmhouse had to be repaired. All it needed was a few bundles of hay set firmly in the patchy places. That too could have been done but then the labourers had not turned up.

For the past eight days, the rain had not let up; the dark clouds had not stirred. Nothing could be seen except a blinding sheet of rain. Nothing could be heard except its deafening *rapa-rapa*. It poured without a moment's respite, the onslaught causing the roof of the farmhouse to leak in many places. The workers must have thatched it badly in the first place because the floor was covered with water.

The previous night, the rain had been simpering a bit but had settled down to a self-assured drizzle early that morning; the clouds looked as grouchy as ever. This was the right time to repair the roof but the men had not come. They had to celebrate their Mirugi *habba*.

Ganapayya had heard the drumbeats from beyond the farm since the previous night. He went out alone towards the areca palms. Even as he walked down the slope, he saw the Sharavathi. Previously, before the dam had risen, the rivers flow was towards the waterfall. Now he could see the water but not the flow. With the dam blocking its way it had stopped right there beside their hillock, restless and choppy. Just the previous week he could see the tips of the boulders on the hill. The water had not risen much. But now it had widened the riverbed on the side away from the hill and was threatening to overflow the bank. The Sharavathi lay like a pregnant woman, full and ready for birthing.

The workers who had come the previous day had said that water stood on the other side of the hill. So it seemed certain that it would surround the hill as the monsoon progressed. After that, no one would be able to venture this way. It was eight days since Krishnayya had sent word that he would be coming. Why had he not come? It would be good if he came before Hosamanehalli became an island.

A lime tree floated, wrenched out by its roots. A few banana plants too had met with the same fate. The water in the pond had eroded a part of the bund to the farm and so one of the areca palms was in danger of falling. As Ganapayya crossed the bridge and turned towards the house, he heard someone calling him. He turned to see Krishnayya.

'Oho! Come, come....'

Krishnayya jumped down from the farmlands to the bridge which shook a bit under his weight.

'Bavayya, did you think I wasn't coming?' he asked.

Ganapayya noticed Krishnayya's attractive moustache and felt a twinge of envy.

'Naturally! Arre, when did you send word you were coming? And why have you taken so long?'

'What could I do, Bava? I was all set to come here eight days ago but Yajamanaru wanted me to see to something in Sagara. I thought that job would take me two days. But it took eight. Anyway, I'm glad I could come at least today. Or else I would've had to swim to your village from the Aralagodu bridge.'

'Why?'

'Don't you know? The Sharavathi is girdling your village from either side. In another four days Hosamanehalli will become an island.'

'Really? Has water risen behind the mountain?'

'Yes Bava. The water's rising from both the sides of the hill. The walkway to Aralagodu isn't covered yet only because it's on a higher level. If the water keeps rising like this, even that pathway will be flooded.'

'Hmm ... just as I feared! Did you go to the house before coming here?'

'No, Bava, I saw you walking towards the farm and so I came here right away.'

'Come, let's go home. She's been waiting for you since these eight days.'

Ganapayya walked up the valley with Krishnayya. A few stray sunbeams peeped weakly from behind the clouds.

Nagaveni had been cleaning rice in a winnowing-fan. But instead of throwing away the paddy she was throwing away grains of rice absent-mindedly. And then, looking at the white grains of rice on the black floor she scolded herself, 'Thu, what's got into me?' and picked up all the rice grains she could and put them back.

These days she was bored in Hosamane. Fortunately for her, her father-in-law kept her company. Or else being in the house would have become tedious. Working on the farm and field had lost its charm as she had to work alone like an owl. Of course, Ganapayya worked alongside. He did say a word or two. But even then, it was not like working together with a group of people. There was a feeling of isolation now. Her husband was taciturn by nature. He spoke only when he was in the mood, not otherwise. And even when he did, there was no intimacy, no companionship she could bank on. It was just so much and not anymore. She was never quite sure if it was sheer indifference or a real contempt that made him keep his distance from her.

Earlier someone or the other would visit them. Herambha's wife or Prameshwarayya's wife would come and talk about this, that, or the other. The Hasalaru women would stand beyond the back door or near the awning and talk about things happening in their lives. Now all of them had gone away. The Deervu women from Aralagodu had not come that way for ages now. At least if they had come, Nagamani would have felt there were some people around. But now she was oppressed by a sense of loneliness.

'It's eight days since Krishnayya sent word to say he's coming,' she thought, 'and he hasn't come yet. I waited for him today, hoping he'd be here. If he comes, I can at least get some news from home. And I won't feel so lonely either. We've grown up together after all. If he comes, I'll surely be rid of this maddening boredom.'

Nagaveni finished cleaning the rice. She put it away and went into the bathroom. Water was flowing with a melodious *julu-julu* into the cauldron from the drain cut out of areca stems. She took water in a *chembu*, tucked her sari a little higher, washed her feet, and came inside the house.

'Koose!' called her father-in-law from the platform outside the front door, 'Who's that talking?'

Nagaveni stiffened. Previously there was no need for such questions. Where there was a village, there had to be people coming and going and talking. Not only the people who lived in it, sometimes those who had to cross the Sharavathi went past the house. Farm hands from Aralagodu too went by on their way to and from work. But now there was dread hovering about, a fear of strangers in the vicinity and questions like 'Who?' 'Why?' entered the head.

When Nagaveni came to the front door and strained her ears towards the voices, she discerned Krishnayya's louder voice even before her husband's.

'Looks like Krishnayya's come, Mava,' she said. And as soon as she was sure it was him, she darted beyond the awning to see him cross the bridge. Krishnayya saw her and waved. The tender leaves of a pepper creeper fluttered coquettishly in the breeze.

'I thought you'd never come,' she said as he climbed the steps to the open veranda. 'Is everyone well at home?'

Krishnayya laughed his loud laugh, put his bag on the platform beside the old man, and brought his palms together to greet Duggajja with a namaskara.

'Thatha, how're you? How's your health now?' he asked the old man in his deep voice.

'As well as I can be. My wheezing's no better. The rains scare me. But tell me, how's everyone at home?'

'They're well, Thatha. Yajamanaru thinks of you quite often. He says you should be taken to Talaguppa or Sagara. He feels medicines from those towns could make you better.'

'Doctors and medicines are just illusions, like smearing oil on a tree with wood-rot. Will a lifespan that's moving forwards ever run backwards?' Then turning to his daughter-in-law who was gawking at Krishnayya, Duggajja said, 'Koose, you're just standing there ... go, bring him some water.'

Nagaveni brought him water to wash his feet before entering the house.

'Krishnayya, go and have a bath,' said Ganapayya, coming from inside. Krishnayya took a panche from his bag and went into the house.

'How's the pain in Amma's waist?' Nagaveni asked, stopping him near the kitchen as he was going to the bathroom.

'She seems to be a little better now. The vaidya from Talaguppa had given her some herbal oil. Massaging with it seems to have helped.'

Nagaveni had not forgotten that her mother had said her lower-back was stiff with pain.

'Has Nagaraja come home?' Nagaraja was her younger brother. He was doing his High School in Sagara.

'No', shouted Krishnayya from the bathroom, 'He may come next week.'

As she heard the water splashing off his back, Nagaveni turned her attention to the smoky fireplace.

'Is dinner ready?' asked Ganapayya, coming into the kitchen.

'The curry is ready. I've got to cook rice. Couldn't you have brought four banana leaves as you were coming in from the farm? We don't have any on which to serve dinner.'

'Did you tell me to get some? Or did I have to dream that you didn't have any?'

'So what? You can get some now, can't you?'

'Oho, I can get some, of course ... as if I'm a servant in her father's house to get some....'

The fire lit up suddenly and Ganapayya moved back with a start. Nagaveni looked at his face in the glow.

He was not teasing her; he seemed irritated about something.

'Don't worry, Krishnayya will get them,' she said to pacify him.

Ganapayya stalked out of the kitchen, hungry and angry.

Clouds covered the sun but there was no rain. Only the wind blew fiercely and there was the distant sound of thunder. But the clouds were low-lying, a sure sign of rain. After dinner Ganapayya took Krishnayya and went out of the house. He had not forgotten what Krishnayya had told him; that Sharavathi was tightening her grip around the Parvatha. Only the road to Aralagodu might be spared.

Ganapayya was frightened that this road too would be engulfed. They should be starting on the next phase of work in the fields and on the farms. What if the labourers from Aralagodu could not come?

Ganapayya walked with Krishnayya along the path to Aralagodu. When they climbed the hillock from one side and went over to the other, they could see the river. It had never come this far. Previously, Sharavathi would flow, hugging a side of the mountain, never straying from her path. But now that her flow was blocked further down, she had begun to spread out, encroaching the neighbouring forest and valley. Trees, shrubs, and bamboo were already knee-deep in rain water, in red muddy water, still and silent.

Ganapayya looked at Krishnayya.

'See how high the water has risen in the past three days. There's no doubt the Parvatha will be marooned in the next three. It'll become an island. And then?'

'Don't worry, Bavayya, I'll see to the work on the field and farm. You don't worry about anything....'

'Who ever thought the government would bring us to this state, Ayya? They've sent everyone else from this village to other places compensating them substantially. But they didn't do anything in my case.... To whom can I now go and talk about our troubles?'

Ganapayya grumbled as if to himself.

'Come, Bavayya, let's go home. It looks like rain.'

Krishnayya took Ganapayya home. The rain was virtually on their heels as they stepped onto the veranda.

That rain poured continuously for eight days.

Aridhraa

'Survive the Aridhraa, you're sure of a harvest'; the proverb kept running in Krishnayya's head as he walked back from Aralagodu. As if the Mirugi rain was not enough, the Aridhraa came pelting down. It was almost impossible to get labourers from Aralagodu to work on the farm. Herambha's seedlings had to be planted. Ganapayya had seeded his fields directly to save the bother of transplanting. But then, his fields had to be weeded. And palm sheaths had to be tied around the arecanut fronds. Though Krishnayya was willing to see to everything, Ganapayya had insisted that they should get help from Aralagodu.

The Sharavathi had already begun to engulf Sita Parvatha but had spared the pathway to Aralagodu. As there was a bulge behind the hillock attached to the Aralagodu hill, water had yet to rise at least five to six feet before it could cover it. So the road from Hosamane to Aralagodu was safe even though expanses of water had formed deep pools on either side of it. Taking advantage of the accessibility, Ganapayya got men from Aralagodu and hastily got the work on the farm and field done. But it was not easy; it took all his patience to cajole them to walk through the rising water to Hosamane. They finally consented only when he raised their wages by eight annas per day.

By the time the fields were weeded, Duggajja was unable to rise from his bed. The wheezing worsened day by day. The old man was hardly aware of what was happening around him. All they could hear was a groan or two from time to time. His condition deteriorated further. Krishnayya went to Aralagodu and got some herbal medicine from a local doctor. Nothing worked. As the Aridhraa rain entered its third phase, Duggajja breathed his last.

Krishnayya went out to see if he could find someone through whom he could send word to others but he had to turn back halfway. The deluge that had forced her way through the Sharavathi was now roaring around Sita Parvatha.

They cremated the old man in front of the cave atop the hill. Ganapayya lit the funeral pyre in a fine drizzle. Krishnayya stood to one side with his arms folded. Nagaveni stood behind him. The rain stopped as the pyre caught fire and waited until it burnt itself down to ashes. It started only when the three turned their backs to the cave and wended their way back home.

The land had become indifferent to the monsoon. Only the pouring rain and the sweeping wind had life in them. Everything else crouched in fear of the ravaging downpour like the bald boulders on the crest of Sita Parvatha. The saplings in the fields stood breathing in the water as it flowed from field to field to join the river. They were barely as tall as a span as they shivered in the onslaught of wind and rain, yet they stood breathing in the slush.

The first sacrifice to the fury of the monsoon was the areca farm. The palms and the banana leaves took the force of the pelting raindrops. The palms that tore away from the trunk with the onslaught of every gust of wind, the trees that came crashing down with them, the pepper creepers that had relied on the tree trunks and the leaves floating in water, everything spoke of the havoc the rains were spreading. Amidst this death, only the pond was rejuvenated. It had been sighing with suffocation during the summer but was now gurgling with laughter, returning water to the Sharavathi a hundredfold.

Water was cascading in torrents from Sita Parvatha too. The steady trickle of rainwater from the roof was all that could be collected for Ganapayya's bathroom as the spring in the hill was now a pond and there were a hundred rivulets streaming out of this pond. All the water headed towards the river.

The Sharavathi was swelling by the moment. Parameshwarayya's lands, hugging a bank, were already inundated. Herambha's lands were not very far away from the river; barely the distance between the outstretched arms of ten men. If the water rose any further, it was quite likely that the water from the river would rush into his field instead of the other way around.

Water had encircled Sita Parvatha. From a distance, Hosamanehalli looked like an island, like an insignificant rock in the sea, a helpless piece of land surrounded by a watery girdle with no contact with the outside world whatsoever.

Parameshwarayya's lands were under water. His house and the house of his labourer, Hala, had caved in, waiting to be washed away. Even Herambha's house and his Byra's house were on their way to desolation. The only things standing were Herambha's and Ganapayya's lands and Ganapayya's house was the only house.

And all it contained was the thatched awning; the veranda with a platform to one side, two dark cave-like rooms, a kitchen, an open bathroom at the back, a cowshed, a shack to stock wood, Ganapayya, on the veranda leaning against the wall, Krishnayya seated on the floor, leaning against a pillar, and Nagaveni walking in and out of the house seeing to her chores. The last three were the only people in Hosamanehalli.

Krishnayya got up and walked down the veranda along the edge of the thatched roof to keep from getting wet. He went to a side and spat out the betel leaf and nut he was chewing. He stood a while watching its red mingle with the brown of the muddy water, and hoisting his maunji over his panche, returned to sit against the pillar in the veranda and faced Ganapayya.

'Bavayya, when do the new rains start? From this Sunday?'

'It's eleven days since the Aridhraa rains began, isn't it? Yes, Punarvasu is from Sunday. But let's see if it brings its rain or not.'

'I only hope it'll give us some respite. How does it expect people to survive this onslaught? Shouldn't we get some rest, day or night?' Krishnayya picked up a small twig and talked, cleaning his teeth.

'Ayyo, let the rain be, Maaraaya. It's that cursed dam!' Ganapayya snapped, 'What shall we do if the stagnating water doesn't sink? We're caught here, aren't we? Suppose something happens to us, what'll be our fate?'

'We're our only help, Bavayya. Either we make a raft or we swim across.'

'I really don't know what to do.'

Ganapayya sat with his head in his hands. He was weighed down with worries he could not handle. He had never felt so helpless ever before. His spirit trembled every time it struck him afresh that they were not in touch with the world outside.

The water in the river had to subside someday, if not today or tomorrow. There was enough to eat for the next four to five months. Work on the lands was done. The two of them could see to the odds and ends; they did not need help from Aralagodu. The fear was not for any of these reasons. It was only because water had surrounded them and isolated them from the rest of the world.

Whenever water stood in the neighbouring forests and valleys during monsoon, wild animals would come towards Sita Parvatha, seeking refuge. And now foxes, deer, and wild goats strolled fearlessly behind the house looking for shelter. A python crept into the wood-shack beside the kitchen. Rabbits scurried about the veranda. The cattle had mooed restlessly a few nights earlier. Nagaveni said she had heard the low oomphs and coughs of a tiger near the cattleshed before dawn. She could be right; perhaps that was why the cattle were restive. Wild animals like the tiger, cheetah, bison, and wild boar lived in the Malenadu forests but they lived in their own territory most of the time. Now with all the extra water around they could be scared too. Ganapayya became even more apprehensive because of their presence. A tiger entered Ganapayya's heart as he sat with his head in his hands.

'Krishnayya, do you know – Nagu heard a tiger roaring near the cattleshed?' he said, turning towards him.

'Really? When?'

'Early this morning. Last night the cows and calves were mooing. They must've seen the tiger.'

Nagaveni had come outside to do something but stood there on hearing talk about the tiger.

'You know, Krishnayya, there's a tiger on the prowl, that's for sure. I heard it clearly this morning.'

'From which side did you hear it?'

'From the back of the house. There's one in the jungles of Hidamba. The farm hands from Alaragodu used to talk about a tiger in that area. Couldn't that same tiger have come here, now that its forest is drowned?'

'Yes, Bavayya, what she says could be true. That tiger could have come this way for protection. We've got to be careful. If it's eyeing our cattleshed, it means danger is lurking very near. Tonight we must secure the door of the shed firmly.'

'Yes, we should.'

'Bavayya, don't you have a gun?'

'No, Maaraaya, I don't. Herambha had one. I didn't keep any. Maybe I should've got one too.'

'Krishnayya, do you know how to shoot?' This was from Nagaveni. She was curious. She had never seen him handling a gun. How did he get to learn anything at all about it?

'I? I learnt quite recently. Padavagoud Basappa taught me. I even shot him a wild boar as *gurudakshine*!'

Nagaveni laughed.

'We could've taken care of the tiger too ... if only we had a gun', Krishnayya said softly as if speaking to himself, 'we've got to be wary.'

That night Krishnayya himself went and locked the door of the cattle shed. It was quite some time since Ganapayya had had his dinner and had gone to bed. The lamp shone faintly on the dividing wall between the rooms. Black soot covered the top half of the chimney like a crown and the wall near the chimney too had a black streak. As Krishnayya got his blanket and settled down to sleep, Nagaveni came out after finishing her chores in the kitchen.

'Sleepy, Krishnayya?'

'How can I be sleepy this early? ... Are you done for the day?'

'Done!'

Wiping her hands on the pallu of her sari, Nagaveni went inside. Then she came out. Her husband was snoring. She sat on the threshold and drew the plate of betel leaves and nuts towards her.

'Want to chew?' she asked.

'No, my eyes are burning.' Krishnayya yawned as he sat leaning against a wall.

Nagaveni tossed a betel nut into her mouth, clipped the stalk of a betel leaf, smeared some sunna on it, and started chewing it.

'Wonder which *raavu* has got hold of this rain!' she exclaimed vehemently.

The rain was unrelenting. And besides, there was the wind. The Aridhraa rains poured without a pause. They had hoped Aridhraa would be mild since Mrigashira had been virulent, but there was no sign of it diminishing. In fact, Aridhraa seemed to be competing with Mrigashira with a will to win.

'Why? Shouldn't it rain during the rainy season? Is the sun supposed to shine? As long as the water doesn't rise till here and drown the village, we're safe,' Krishnayya countered.

'Who knows what'll happen, Krishnayya? I told him, "Let's not worry about the compensation from the government. We'll think about it later. For now, let's get away from here." But he wouldn't listen to me. Mava too didn't want us to move out. Appayya wouldn't have said anything if we'd spent these four months with them. He could've gone to the office a few more times, seen this man and that, and had got the money and lands due to us. But he'll do only what *he* wants to do. Somebody told him the village wouldn't drown this year. And so he decided we should stay on. Mava died here. That was his wish, anyway. Who knows what else is awaiting us? Tigers, foxes, snakes, and boars have started living behind our house.'

Krishnayya could not bear the heaviness in Nagaveni's voice. And yet he could understand her husband's pig-headedness. He knew how Ganapayya felt about moving in with his father-in-law even if it was for a mere four months. He had spoken to Krishnayya about the delicacy of the situation. Also, he was not sure if the government would really compensate him after the monsoon. If he left the saplings he had planted and went to live with his wife's family, what would they eat later? And if the government let him down, would he have to live on his father-in-law's bounty for a year? This was Ganapayya's unspoken fear. But how could a woman like Nagaveni understand all this?

Krishnayya got up from where he was sitting and went forward. When Nagaveni pushed the plate of betel leaves and nuts towards him he took it and sat down.

'What's the point in weeping now, Nagu?' he said, 'Bavayya didn't want to throw away the morsel of food in his hand. And so he's stayed on. What can we do about it now? Yes, there's water surrounding the village. But can we move from here? We have to stay and face whatever comes, shouldn't we? Why are you scared? Bavayya's here, I'm here. Be brave.'

'It's easy for you to take his side, Krishnayya. My heart keeps trembling day and night. I'm gripped with so many fears: What will happen when? What if water rushes into the house? What if the tiger or a boar comes in and takes away one of us? Of course, I do feel a little braver because you're here. I'd have died by now if you hadn't come.'

'Ayyo, you silly girl! With two men in the house, will we leave a woman to the tiger?' Krishnayya laughed at her heartily.

Nagaveni sat staring at his reddened lips and his arms and chest heaving with laughter. She felt comforted to hear him; more restful, much like coming to a cool shady place after a long blistering walk in the hot summer sun. She wondered why she found Krishnayya's presence and his chatter so pleasing, so reassuring. Why did she want to keep staring at him, to sit with him? Why did her heart jump with joy whenever she caught sight of him? What could be the reason?

Perhaps the zing of the betel nut had got to her head or the bit of tobacco had made her lightheaded. Nagaveni felt like stretching out right where she was. How nice it would be if Krishnayya were to sit closer and she could rest her head on his lap and go to sleep. 'Previously I used to touch him with such ease, even beat him. I was quite comfortable touching him until I was about twelve-thirteen. Only Amma would tell me it was not the right thing to do. But since I got married Krishnayya's gone far from me; very far....' Her thoughts meandered on.

She felt resentful, agitated. Krishnayya's comforting words made room for other thoughts to surface; thoughts she had never thought before. She wanted to tell him she was not happy here. She wanted to rest her head on his chest and weep. She looked up.

'Get up, Nagu. Go and sleep,' said Krishnayya and going to his bed, he lay down and drew the blanket over his head.

Nagaveni sat on for a while on the threshold, soothing her ruffled emotions and then got up.

'What's come over me? Why are these crazy feelings running through me? Why have I got so fond of Krishnayya lately? How could I've forgotten my husband sleeping in the inner room?'

She got up in a hurry, took the wall lamp and went into the room. She closed the door, bolted it, and hung the lamp on a nail on the wall and turned towards her husband's bed. That was when she was aware of his two red eyes, wide open and staring at her. She felt as if someone had thrown smouldering ember at her.

'Are you done with talking?' The question felt like the sting of a rap on a tethered calf.

'Yes ... why?'

'Just asked ... you could've gone on longer, couldn't you?' Nagaveni put off the lamp and got into bed. As she drew up her blanket to cover her face, she heard Ganapayya's, 'You're going beyond the limit these days.'

Nagaveni was in no mood to talk. She turned over to the other side. The cot creaked. The rats in the granary scampered down. Ganapayya clenched his fists and cleaved the darkness with his stare.

When Nagaveni had come into the room earlier Ganapayya had just finished his first round of sleep. He had expected her to return with the lamp. But she had not come. She had sat with Krishnayya instead, chewing betel leaves with him. And then they got chatting. Though he could not make out what they were talking about because of the rain, Ganapayya was furious that she wanted to talk to him at all.

'This isn't anything new, it was always like this. There was a spring in her step every time we talked about Krishnayya. And she's been moving about the house with a new verve ever since he came to stay. How much she talks to him, how much she laughs with him. Why? Is he her elder brother? He's just an orphan her father brought home and looked after. Where's the need to be so familiar with him? Why?'

He had thought of slapping her as soon as she came in from chatting with Krishnayya. But he controlled himself with great difficulty. After all Nagaveni was his wife. It was not good for him to distrust her so easily. He should wait and see. And so he had swallowed his overflowing wrath and merely said, 'You're going beyond the limit.' But it sounded like a whiplash.

He turned towards her but Nagaveni had deliberately moved farther from him. 'If she can be so insolent, can't I be much more?' he said to himself as he turned away from her.

But for the sound of the wind and rain, there was silence. The cold mountain air from Sita Parvatha breezed through the whole house.

Punarvasu

By the time Saturday evening made way for Sunday morning, the sun was shining brightly. The rain had tucked in all signs of sound and fury and the sky was as clean as a well-swept front yard. Except for a few puddles here and there, the floor started drying in the front porch, the backyard and the awning. Birds flew about in the tender sunlight. Wildfowl and hare scurried about from shrubs and thickets. Sounds of *keech-keech* came from the birds in Sita Parvatha. The cattle, tired of being cooped up in the byre, stretched out their necks and stared at the sun.

Now they were sure the Punarvasu rain would give them an eight-day respite. Krishnayya tightened a girdle round his waist, stuck his knife through it, and went towards the farm. Ganapayya slung a spade over his shoulder and set out towards the fields. Nagaveni felt light-hearted as she went about her work.

The rains had not created much havoc in Ganapayya's farm. There were a few new potholes where water had eroded the bank and had formed small pools. An areca palm that had been teetering for quite some time had fallen. One or two saplings too were washed away and a few banana plants were destroyed. By the time Krishnayya wandered around the farm and came towards the field, Ganapayya was standing on a low ridge and surveying it.

Even here there was no damage to speak of. Water flowed from one field to the other. The shoots were a rich green. They stood in the slush and swayed in the morning breeze that came in gentle waves to tickle them. A gentle sunlight pervaded the field

'How's the farm?' asked Ganapayya.

'Nothing much has happened there, Bava. Remember the areca palm near the bridge? Only *that* has fallen.'

Both of them walked towards Herambha's farm. The wind had wrecked some havoc there. A few trees were uprooted. The water from the pond had gushed into the farm and had washed away the sheaths that protected the fronds. As they trudged towards Herambha's paddy field, Ganapayya groaned, 'Ayyo!' The Sharavathi had forced her way into the field, submerging the low-lying area hugging her bank. But, at least, the rest of the field was safe.

Krishnayya noticed the river water; it was thick and slushy.

'Bavayya, the water won't rise any higher,' he said.

'How can you tell?' asked Ganapayya, staring at him.

'Listen to that noise in the distance. Isn't that the sound of water overflowing from the dam? The wall's about ninety to a hundred feet high now. So, it's holding that much of water and releasing only the rest. Bavayya, we've won the battle!' he exclaimed.

Ganapayya too felt he had won the battle this monsoon.

The Sharavathi was flowing forward in slow motion. So it meant that water would not stagnate in pools. He could let go of the fear that the village would drown.

'Yes, you're right!' Ganapayya nodded.

The two of them walked home in companionable silence, happy they had survived the trial by water.

As they entered the veranda, they saw Nagaveni standing on the platform, crying.

'Krishnayya! ... In the kitchen ... a snake!'

'What? A snake?' Ganapayya stepped back voluntarily.

'Where?' said Krishnayya rushing into the house.

Resting its tail over the threshold to the kitchen was a water-snake, sleeping peacefully. The rest of its body was hidden somewhere in the kitchen.

'Here, hit it! It's not a cobra, Krishnayya. It's just a water-snake,' said Ganapayya bringing a long stick and handing it to him.

Krishnayya pushed him aside, signalled to Nagaveni to move away, and holding the snake by the tail, he twisted it once round his hand and gave it a quick tug. A five feet long snake emerged and hung squirming in his grip. Holding the snake high above his head Krishnayya ran towards the backyard. He swung the snake aloft briskly four times and flung it into the distance. It flew skywards, fell with a splash, slithered, and righted itself. Krishnayya caught hold of it again and tossed it again the same way. The snake fell into the bushes beyond the yard.

Nagaveni threw him an admiring look as she went inside.

After lunch Krishnayya went out for a stroll. He felt tied down with the constant rain. He wanted a long walk in the sun and so took the road from Hosamane to Aralagodu. He walked towards the Sita Parvatha. Because there were hardly any people going up the hill these days, the pathway was covered over with grass; he could not make out the way to the top. He climbed a bit of Sita Parvatha and then got down on the other side. He had scarcely walked ten steps when he saw water. He stopped. It was like a waterfall. There was water everywhere; to the right, to the left, wherever he looked. It had spread out for over a furlong in front of him. And beyond it, in the distance, was the green hill of Aralagodu with its houses and fields. But on this side of the bridge he could see only the top of submerged trees. The water was at least ten feet high. Will this water ever dry up? When?

Krishnayya walked into the water gingerly. There were a few carcasses floating about: rabbits, wildfowl, deer. He could hardly make them out; they were that bloated. They might have drowned in the water or might have died in the wind and rain. They were putrefied and stinking. He thought it was not wise to go on. He turned towards the pathway that was submerged in water and walked back to the village.

When Ganapayya sent word for him, Krishnayya had not been keen on going. In any case, Nagaveni's father had not asked him to go and he felt it was not for him to take a decision. But then, Ganapayya had sent word to his father-in-law too asking for Krishnayya and he had said, 'Krishna, the girl's husband has sent for you. Go and spend these four months with them.' Hoping to escape the situation, Krishnayya had even gone to Sagara on some pretext but as soon as he returned after eight days, his master said, 'Go now'.

And so he had come to Hosamane.

'Nagaveni is Yajamanaru's daughter, ten years younger to me', he mused, 'I've carried her, played with her, and helped her grow.... In those days we always spent time together eating, sleeping, playing. Even as she was growing up, I was fascinated with her. I've noticed her firm breasts under her blouse, her arms filling out, her reddened cheeks, her slender swaying waist. I've wanted to be with her all the time, teasing her, making her cry, making her laugh, comforting her, just being with her. It was a longing, a craze. But her mother would always keep an eye on us, watching over us like an eagle.

'Krishna, Nagu is a big girl now. Don't call her to play with you as you used to do,' she'd say. She must've said something similar to Nagu too.

'Nagu moved from skirts and blouses to saris. Those breasts were covered with a pallu. Yajamanaru got busy with getting his daughter married. The wedding too happened. I had gone right up to the Talaguppa bus stand to see her off. How much she cried when the bus was to leave! I too wept. I couldn't eat the next day. Once when she came home, her mother told her about it and laughed.

'I used to come here once in a way. During my first visit we had climbed right to the cave on Sita Parvatha. But since then I've tried hard to forget Nagaveni. After all, she's my master's daughter. She's married. I'd decided I shouldn't be hankering after her.

'But now, I'm caught in the web once again.

'Nagaveni forgets herself when I'm around. She's not aware that her husband's around. She doesn't need anything else when I'm with her; she's that preoccupied. But who knows where this will lead us? How will Ganapayya view the way we're comfortable with each other? Should I tell her not to be so brash?'

But Krishnayya's selfishness prevented him from asking Nagaveni to be circumspect. He wanted her to behave as she did; to talk excitedly, to laugh helplessly in his presence, to ignore her husband while *he* was around. It gave him a certain pleasure and satisfaction.

This is what he wanted but, at the same time, he did not want to ruin her life. Could the two go hand in hand?

He would have liked to return home. But how? They were hedged in by water that had risen to the level of the tree-tops. And besides, his master had asked him to spend four months with them.

Krishnayya could not sort out his problem.

He came down the hill and started homewards. He took out his girdle, placed it on the platform, and went inside. Nagaveni slipped into the kitchen holding the pallu of her sari to her eyes. She was weeping. Ganapayya strode out looking like thunder.

'Where had you gone?' he asked gruffly.

'I went up to the hill to see if I could return home if the water had gone down,' said Krishnayya in ill-concealed anguish, 'but the pathway is drowned in water ... I'll have to swim to the other bank.'

'Hmm, ... no need to think about that now. Go and see to the cattle. You can go when the water level sinks.'

Ganapayya replaced his frown with a smile but Krishnayya did not respond to it. He could hear Nagaveni sobbing in the kitchen. He dragged his feet towards the cattle shed.

Krishnayya went out again after lunch. Nagaveni came out of the kitchen wiping her hands on her sari. She did not find him on the veranda.

'You know, where's Krishnayya?' she asked as usual. Ganapayya burst into flame like chaff that had been ignited.

'Who's that *bewarsi* to you?' And even before she could say something, he pounced on her, 'If you bring up his name again, I'll hack you down. Take care. I'll break your legs if you walk about in front of him; slit your tongue if you talk to him.'

Nagaveni felt disgusted to hear her husband rave like a low-class man. She was furious too that he could talk to her that way.

'Do what you please', she said calmly, 'Krishnayya's my kinsman.'

Ganapayya was roused even more. He dragged her inside and beat her until he had no strength left.

And then he felt sick; he could not believe he had stooped so low.

'Go and die!' he said and leaned against the bed.

By the time Krishnayya returned, Ganapayya had caught a nap. Nagaveni was still crying. Anger flared up in Ganapayya on seeing Krishnayya but it simmered down and he could talk to him, smile at him. He felt bad that he had created an unnecessary ruckus. As Krishnayya went to the cattle shed, Ganapayya took his knife and went down to the farm.

Krishnayya opened the door of the byre and came towards the house. He saw Ganapayya cross the bridge and go towards the farm and went inside.

'What happened, Nagu?' he asked.

Nagaveni leaned against the kitchen door and wailed afresh. Her unkempt hair, broken bangles, swollen eyes, and her gasping sobs told him everything.

'Did Bava beat you?'

In those days, whenever her mother beat her or her father scolded her, he would ask similar questions. He would comfort her, tickle her, make her laugh. But now?

'I know the reason, Nagu ... I came to help you out only because I couldn't say "no" to your father. Even now I'm ready to go back.'

'It's not your fault at all, Krishnayya. I beg of you. Don't talk of going back. That's his nature. He takes everything seriously.'

'No, Nagu. It isn't his fault at all. *We* shouldn't be so easy-going with each other. Whatever it be, you're *his* wife now. If you talk to me or laugh at whatever I say, he'll naturally feel slighted. Nagu, I haven't come here to ruin your life. I'll stay only if both you and Bava want me to stay. But please don't favour me over him in any way.'

Krishnayya spoke to her like the turbulent river and walked away. Nagaveni stood transfixed as if she had seen her own state of mind.

Krishnayya put on his slippers and went towards the farm.

Ganapayya cut banana leaves, rolled them together in a neat bundle, and headed homewards when he saw Krishnayya walking towards him. He looked grim, purposeful. Ganapayya was filled with fear. Krishnayya could break his bones if he as much as punched him. He was, after all, lanky like a wind-swept tree with not much sap in his body. He thought it would be dangerous to confront Krishnayya. But then again, how could he sit back and watch Nagaveni with this man? How much of a man was *he* if he could not bring his wife to her senses?

Krishnayya met him on the bund.

'Bavayya.'

It sounded like the hiss of a wounded cobra. Krishnayya's eyes were red.

'Bavayya, it isn't fair that you distrust Nagu just because she talks to me the way she does. We've grown up together ... she's like my sister. If you suspect her, it's like you spitting into your drinking water. I came here only to help you out, not for any other reason. If I did have any such heinous desires, it wouldn't be difficult for me to fulfil them. If you don't want me here, tell me so, I'll go back. I'm staying only because I don't know how to explain this to Yajamanaru. This water as deep at the hight of ten men is nothing for me. If you hurt Nagu in any way again, I'll go back without telling you.'

Ganapayya stuck his knife into his girdle and shifted the bundle of banana leaves to the other shoulder. He was struck by the quiet dignity with which Krishnayya had spoken. His words were as impressive as his appearance. The gravity of what Krishnayya had said was enough to shake him up. Faint beads of sweat shone on Ganapayya in the frail monsoon sun. He knew he could not find fault with whatever Krishnayya had said.

'Whatever's happened has happened, Krishnayya. She hasn't been this way before ... I too lost my cool ... Come, let's go back home.'

Both of them crossed the bridge together.

***

'When he asked me what that bewarsi was to me, jumping up and down as if he had stuck his hand in a beehive, it's true I said he was my kinsman.' Nagaveni said to herself, 'I do think he's like an elder brother. But I can't accept that truth all the time; I only said so to quell his suspicion. Krishnayya's truly my companion. As soon as I hear his name, my heart lights up like those different coloured matchsticks we light for Deepavali. It showers sparkles like a hundred flower-pots lit together. It arches like the rainbow from heaven to earth and sets me afire.

'Krishnayya too said something to me before he went out. I'm sure it's come only from the tip of his tongue. It's come so that my husband may not ill-treat me, so that I may not be hurt. But I know what's in his heart. I know he too longs to talk to me, to be near me.'

Nagaveni saw Krishnayya like an aura pervading everything around her. She felt disgust for her husband, repulsion, contempt.

'I've reached a point where I *don't* want to live with my husband. I want Krishnayya. I don't care whether it's dharma or adharma, right or wrong. My spirit longs for Krishnayya and it will not rest until I have him.

'But how ...?

Will my husband let me? Will Krishnayya agree? What will Amma say? What will Appa do? Brothers, sisters, people from our town, from Aralagodu, other friends and relatives? When I think of them, my mind cringes. Instead of being so shameless, why shouldn't I drown myself in the Sharavathi?'

Nagaveni arranged splinters in the fireplace and lit them. She sat with her chin on her hand staring at the tongues of fire that looked like a nude stretching her arms and legs seductively towards the pieces of wood.

She wondered if she was going astray. Ganapayya had taken her hand in marriage with fire as witness. How could she deceive him? She got up from there.

By the time Ganapayya and Krishnayya returned, Nagaveni had washed her face.

Pushya

The rains beleaguered them after an eight-day respite. Dark clouds cast their gloom and the wind howled like one possessed. The cattle that had been wandering about returned to the shed. Krishnayya brought in banana and betel leaves to last for eight days.

As the rain thundered down, he sat on the platform and chewed betel leaves one after the other; this was the only way to fight boredom. Most of the villagers played card games to while away the time. But he had not learnt any because playing cards was taboo in his house. Perhaps he would have learnt a few on the sly if he had not been scared of his master but Krishnayya knew he was dead against such games. Of course, there were other indoor games he would play at home like *pagade* and *channamane*. But with whom could he play them here? And in any case, the kits were with Nagaveni and he did not want to play with her.

Previously, she would have called him.

'Krishnayya, let's play pagade, shall we?'

But that was a long time ago; a long, long time ago. Now he did not have the courage to say, 'Yes, let's' even if she did call him.

The rain fell from the roof like a waterfall. It flowed down the hill and from behind the house and jumped down into a pond in the farm. These sounds mingled with that of the wind and rain to deafen everyone.

Ganapayya was inside. He could be asleep. He had the habit of enjoying a siesta after lunch. Nagaveni too would be sleeping. Krishnayya could have caught a nap but somehow he could not bring himself to sleep during the day. He thought it was not proper to cultivate the habit. Was he the master of a household or a landowner or some lord to eat and sleep? He was only a labourer, after all, working for the food he ate and for the corner where he slept. Why should he develop such excesses?

He stood up looking for something to do. The strands of jute that made up the strings of the girdle in which he stuck his knife were frayed in places. So he got some fresh jute and sat down by the edge of the veranda to roll bits of it on his thigh to twist it into strands. Later he would hold the three strands together and twist them to make the three-ply cord for the waistband.

He heard the jingle of bangles. Nagaveni did not talk to him. He carried on the task on hand, pretending he was not aware of her. When he looked up after some time she was not there. He did not know how long she had stood there at the door.

'Naguuuuuu!' his heart screamed, 'You got married. You entered your husband's house. And I thought you were happy. But what kind of a life is this?' He pressed the strands against his thigh in anguish as he rolled them together. The friction scraped the burning skin, making it red and angry. Nagaveni had stopped talking to him. But she was not talking to her husband either. She was silent as if she had lost her tongue. She did not talk, did not laugh; she only moped and grew thinner day by day.

'Nagu, what's happening?' The question came to the tip of his tongue threatening to ask her but stopped short. 'Who am I to ask such questions? It's better I bite my tongue.'

Krishnayya's mind churned. He longed to talk to Nagaveni but he controlled himself; he could not trust himself. He did not want to ruin her life with her husband. He did not want to come in the way of her happiness, her peace of mind. 'But is she really happy with him? Instead of killing her with good intentions what if I go ahead and give her the kind of bliss I *know* I can give her? Why do I hesitate? What's holding me back?' Krishnayya did not know what was right and what was wrong. He was caught between the two.

He could not sit there and twist the cord any longer. He stopped the task midway, hung it on a nail, and went outside. The thatch was leaking in places. The areca sheath that had been spread on it had blown away and water was dripping on the veranda. But it could be repaired only after the rains. So until then they would have to endure the leaky roof. The farm soaked in the rain, the areca trees swayed with abandon with their palms all askew. The areca fronds bound with sheath swung to and fro with the force of the wind.

'I won't be here to harvest the areca nuts. I shouldn't be here. As soon as the rain stops, as soon as water level in the Sharavathi drops and people start coming this way, I'll go back. Anyway, I have fulfilled the purpose I came for.'

For a moment the rain stalled but only for a moment. Then she charged down the valley with such force that she was like a drape let down from sky to earth.

'Thu!' said Krishnayya, 'this rain is no better than the tears of a woman!'

Nagaveni too was like the rain, weeping for the past eight days; her face, the smouldering clouds, dark and angry; her sighs, the moaning wind from Sita Parvatha.

'And I'm the only one enduring her cloudy, rainy, windy depression. Ganapayya seems hardly aware of what could be happening inside her. He's quite cordial to me. But my anguish is tearing at my guts. Should Nagaveni stay this way? Like low-lying dark clouds? Like raindrops blasted by the wind? Like the wind that whizzes down from the crouching boulders? Should she stay this way?'

As a gust of wind sprayed water on the thatched canopy, Krishnayya stepped back into the veranda.

He wanted to do something to keep himself occupied. His eyes wandered over the tiled roof, the beams, the whitewashed walls, the four pegs shaped like parrots, a creeper strung tight like a clothes-line. Towards this end was the cross pole, the girdle to stick the knife, the knife and Ganapayya's *thundu-panche*. At the other end was Nagaveni's blouse, flapping in the wind and soaking in the rain. What was there that he *could* do?

Ganapayya came outside, red-eyed and sleepy. Retying his panche firmly round his waist, he yawned and stretched.

'Ahaha!' he said, hugging himself to keep away the sudden chill.

'O! Is the younger brother raining instead of the elder one?' he asked no one in particular, referring to the rain easing out.

'And what are *you* doing?' he asked Krishnayya and without pausing for a reply said, 'O, that's good!' looking at the strands of jute he had been twisting to make a new girdle. And then, 'Don't you feel sleepy in the afternoons? Sleeping during the day isn't good, anyway.'

Krishnayya did not say anything. He only smiled at Ganapayya standing there with half-closed eyes, scratching his armpits.

Ganapayya went to the edge of the veranda, rinsed his mouth, washed his face with the rainwater from the roof collected in a cauldron, and wiped it with the strip of cloth on the clothes-line.

'Nagu, get us two tumblers of hot coffee,' he called out as he pulled out a mat and sat down.

Krishnayya sat at a little distance and began to work again on the cord for the girdle.

Ganapayya was talking. It was his usual monsoon-grumble: this year the monsoon was not as good as it used to be…. Won't the rains get scantier as forests were cleared?… Malenadu was becoming barren with trees being cut to make way for railway tracks and highways, telegraph lines and dams and townships for outsiders…. If they continued to hack trees at this rate, of course, the rains will get scarce. And there won't be enough water in the Linganamakki Dam. The Sharavathi Project will be a waste….

'Serves them right,' Ganapayya cursed the government.

'I'm glad they didn't compensate me with land elsewhere and money. I've got a good crop in the fields and the farms,' he rejoiced.

'Krishnayya, have you bought any land for yourself?'

'How could I? Yajamanaru has put by a few acres for me.'

'Really? Get married and start a family, Ayya. How long can you stay in someone else's house?'

'I'm thinking of it. Perhaps next year ...'

Nagaveni came with the coffee. She gave her husband a glass and placed another near Krishnayya and was about to go in when Ganapayya shouted, 'Did you hear that, Nagu?'

She stopped in her tracks and looked at her husband questioningly. He gulped down a sip of coffee and said, 'Krishnayya's getting married next summer. You'll get an Athige!'

Nagaveni stubbed her big toe on the threshold to the kitchen. Krishnayya put down the tumbler he had lifted to his lips.

Krishnayya went outside to check on the cattle. He had let them loose for a while as the rain had let up. That was a mistake; all of them had returned after two hours except Belli. The clouds were gathering force for another onslaught. This rain would pour without ceasing for another eight days. Krishnayya tethered the cows and gave them their feed. Where could Belli have gone?

'Bavayya, Belli hasn't comeback,' he said.

Ganapayya leant against a pillar in the veranda pealing the skin off the raw areca nuts.

'Ayyo, that harlot of a cow has this habit, Maaraaya. It isn't anything new she's started now. She was always like that. She goes to the top of the hill and hangs about the cave. I don't know what she finds there. Maybe her mother's *pinda*,' he said, engrossed in what he was doing.

'I'll go and look for her.'

'Do you know the way? Be careful. There'll be plenty of leeches.'

Krishnayya was frightened of leeches latching on and sucking his blood. So he rubbed oil on his legs and set out.

The path to the top of Sita Parvatha had disappeared under an overgrowth of grass. Krishnayya visualized the previous time when he had gone right to the cave with Ganapayya and Nagaveni and climbed in that direction. Trees, shrubs, and creepers had grown as they pleased because people and cattle hardly went up during the monsoon. And these days, Ganapayya was the only person who cut fresh grass for his cattle. The trees had entwined their branches overhead, making the walk in the gloom eerie. Shrubs shivered as wild creatures scurried about. A rabbit hopped here, a wildfowl flew there, a peacock set up a raucous din from the branches of a tree. Krishnayya wondered how these creatures survived in the rain.

But the forestlands did not continue for long. They were only half way up. Then they gave way to grass that made way for huge boulders. Krishnayya knew he was somewhere near the top from where he could get an overview of the whole area. He walked out of the darkness of the forest, away from the creepers that got entangled with his feet and stood on open ground. Right in front was what looked like the sea, a sea of muddy water. There was water everywhere; wherever he looked, to his right, to his left. And in the distance, beyond the water was the Linganamakki Dam and overflowing from it was the cataract that jumped down and rose up as fine mist to become white clouds in the white sky. Floating in the water were hillocks like tiny islands. These were the remnants of huge hills that the water had swallowed up, leaving only the crests.

'Once the dam is completed, *that* will be the state of this hillock too', thought Krishnayya, reaching the top and surveying the view, 'the water will come right up till here. This hill too will drown completely. And with it, Hosamanehalli, Nagaveni's house, the cave, everything with be covered by the waters of the Sharavathi. The water's flowing away now only because the dam isn't ready yet. Who knows how high it would've risen otherwise?'

'Belli ... Come Belli!'

Krishnayya yelled as he walked about, looking this way and that for the cow. He came towards the boulders. He recognized the one on which he had sat when he came with Nagaveni the first time he visited. Tender memories came flooding of her leaning against a black boulder in a green sari and red blouse....

'Abah, I'm exhausted', she had said, wiping her neck, ears, cheeks, and forehead with the pallu of her sari. She had looked lovely.

Krishnayya remembered how he had gazed at her with love, longing, passion, desire! A fire had flared up in him. But only for a moment; it flickered and went out to see Ganapayya standing in front of them. She was now her husband's property. He felt as if he was pouring the water in his cupped hands back into the flowing river. He had backed out. Even now she was an outsider to him; the cool still water he could never drink.

Krishnayya stood beside the boulder for a while, climbed it, and got down on the other side. And there was the cave. And there was Belli lying in front of its gaping mouth.

'Belliiiii, come ... come ... come, Belli,' he called as he went forward but stepped back quickly. Belli was not sleeping. She was lying with her head twisted grotesquely. Blood, red blood lay in huge fresh clots on the green grass.

'Belli!' he groaned.

The white Belli with three or four black patches hardly as big as a palm did not flick her ear; she did not turn to look at him. Instead, he heard a low growl from inside the cave. Krishnayya had bent towards Belli and was caressing her when he felt as if someone had splashed water on him. He straightened, scared. The growl came again, louder. He backed, climbed the boulder, jumped down on the other side and hid there.

But the tiger did not come out of the cave. Krishnayya climbed down the hill as fast as he could, knowing it was not wise to go forward bare-handed.

Ganapayya slumped when he heard the news. He did not mind that Belli was dead; he was worried that the tiger was right behind their house. How could they live there with the tiger so close to them? How could they walk about? How much longer would it stay? It had killed Belli that day. Couldn't it raid the cattle-shed the next day and the house the day after? Fear gripped Ganapayya again.

The tiger had forewarned them that it was in the vicinity. But now that Krishnayya said he had seen the tiger that had killed Belli with his own eyes and heard it with his own ears, Ganapayya was petrified.

'Did you hear, Nagu? Belli was killed by the tiger,' he said.

She looked at him without any expression.

'I would've been rid of a pest if the tiger had taken you instead,' he ranted, 'what with the water closing in on us and wild animals on the prowl, your long face is all I need!'

The rain that was holding up since the morning started again. Krishnayya stood in the veranda listening to Ganapayya. There was no sound from Nagaveni. The rain started slowly but built up to a steady downpour. And darkness covered the land.

Aslesha

Hosamanehalli was hedged in by muddy water. Creatures that lived in burrows, snake-pits, thickets, caves, and hollows of trees came out of their homes, protesting against the gushing waters and having a free run of the place. With no one in sight and no one within earshot from the world beyond the village and with the three of them becoming one too many, Krishnayya's head screamed for company. There was nothing except the whining wind and the rain weeping like an ill-starred woman, and now ...

He could not laugh his hearty laugh or eat a wholesome meal or sleep to forget his troubles. He could not open out his heart to anyone, could not trust anyone, could not embrace anyone as his own. The householder, Ganapayya, could be feeling the same way. Nagaveni too. Each of them felt shackled to a log and forced to carry it on their heads; Krishnayya winced as if a thorn, embedded in his heel, hurt when least expected. Life had become distasteful.

Ganapayya could not trust his wife. She might have said that Krishnayya was like an elder brother. He too might have accepted her as a younger sister. But Ganapayya suspected they had other feelings for each other. She had called out to Krishnayya to kill the snake. She stared at him as if she desired him, as if she would devour him. True, she had stopped talking to him, laughing with him but then, she had stopped talking to her husband too as if he was wrong in taking her to task.

'What else should I do?' thought Ganapayya. 'Is it possible for me to let her to do as she will; to let her be happy with Krishnayya? If I let her be, Nagaveni might do just that. How can *I* live then? Krishnayya lived in her house. Who knows how things were between them before she was married to me? When she asked me to get Krishnayya here for the monsoon, I didn't realize what was afoot. But now I do. Only, I can't see how this'll end. I thought Nagaveni was naive. I trusted her, loved her, desired her. Can she deceive me this way? Krishnayya calls me Bavayya. Can he stab me in the back?'

The poison worked its way slowly but relentlessly. Ganapayya raged at his wife. He became distant with Krishnayya, almost indifferent.

Nagaveni had arrived at her own decision. All the love and trust she had for the creature called her husband had dwindled the moment he said they should not take refuge from the monsoon in her father's house. And when she had to face the fear of flooding, snake, and tiger, she cut herself from him completely. She shut him out of her heart and mind since Krishnayya was somewhere around, anyway. Now her heart throbbed for Krishnayya alone. She longed to be his.

Krishnayya would have gone home if only the water around Hosamane had subsided, if only there were no wild animals on the prowl around the house. He stayed on mainly for Nagaveni's sake, for whatever pleasure she got out of his presence. He stayed even though he felt his friendship with her might jeopardize her family life.

The water surrounding Hosamanehalli did not sink, the fury of the wind did not abate. The Aslesha rain fell day and night.

***

Krishnayya felt someone shaking him awake and opened his eyes. It was pitch dark with not even a needle-point of light. He felt somehow close to him, someone leaning on him, tender fingers running down his face, neck, shoulders.

'Naaguu!'

'Krishnaaa!' whispered Nagaveni lying on his chest with her face close to his.

'Krishna, why are you killing me this way?' Only when she held him in her tight embrace did Krishnayya begin to realize what was happening.

He trembled imagining what could happen if Ganapayya were to see them. He was appalled by their closeness and even thought of slapping Nagaveni for arousing him. But before he could shove her away, Nagaveni's warm delicate body pressed against his, milking his desire for her. He was vaguely aware of gathering all his thoughts together, putting a basket over them, and setting a grinding stone on it. He drew her into his arms; nothing else mattered.

'Nagu!' he whispered in her ear. She wept like the monsoon, heaving and sighing.

He too sobbed with her and a flood of tears washed over them, drowning them in a shared sorrow. The rain roared and the wind from the Sita Parvatha howled with abandon. The rats in the granary *keech-keeched* as they chased each other. Ganapayya's steady snores came all the way from the inner room to touch their backs.

Krishnayya pushed Nagaveni aside and sat up. He pushed at her slim arm as if to push her away. But when she too sat up and leaned against his chest, he groaned.

'Nagu ... what's happened?' he wept.

'Krishna, I can't live without you. I can't live in this house,' she sobbed helplessly.

'No, Nagu, this is not the way you speak. This is your home. Ganapayya's your husband. You *have to* live here ... Your life can't be ruined because of me. I slipped. True. But this is the first time ... and this is the last ... I'm leaving tomorrow morning ... I'm leaving.'

The thoughts on which he had drawn a basket to cover them when he drew Nagaveni close to him had now pushed it aside and stood staring at him. He felt helpless as if he were looking at the tiger.

'Oh, my God! What's happened?' he cried, all in a dither, 'Did the Sharavathi wash over me? Has she surrounded the house? Has she drowned Sita Parvatha? What should I do now?' And turning to Nagaveni said angrily, 'Nagu, you shouldn't have come to this. You shouldn't have cheated on your husband. You shouldn't have made me do something so wrong. It is done. Now, go away.' He pushed her brusquely.

'Krishna, I've attained moksha. I'm ready to drown in the Sharavathi tomorrow. Today, I've got what I wanted,' Nagaveni said, caressing his arm.

Krishnayya sat stunned. He was only vaguely aware of Nagaveni getting up and going away.

'I've attained bliss.... My desire has been fulfilled.... Who said this?' mused Krishnayya, 'Not Nagaveni at all. She has merely taken the words from my heart and spoken them. I don't know if what we did was right or wrong but those few moments were surely bliss. I too felt an "ah!", didn't I? I too am satiated.'

Krishnayya pulled the blanket over himself and slept. The rain sang a lullaby.

He woke up as dawn was breaking. He could not trust himself to stay on. He knew he would have to be party to whatever else might happen.

'It's best I leave now,' he decided, 'it's not very far from the edge of Sita Parvatha to the bridge that leads to the Aralagodu hill. I can swim across. I just have to steer clear of trees and not get my legs entangled in creepers. Anyway, I've told Nagaveni. Ganapayya will understand. I'll think up a lame excuse to tell Yajamanaru. I can't stay here any longer.'

He got up. He crept softly to the door, opened it, and stepped outside. There was a slight drizzle. He walked on getting drenched; he had forgotten his blanket. Then he remembered Nagaveni. Should he stay back with her? Could he continue to pretend to be her elder brother?

'Thu, disgusting! What happened last night was bad enough. It cannot continue,' he walked on.

Krishnayya walked up the back of Sita Parvatha and down the side that led to Aralagodu. He walked into the water. It was cold. He could see the bridge and was sure he could swim the distance. He took out his shirt and panche, tied them to his head and jumped into the water. There was no point in thinking any further.

The flood had no force in it; the water was quite calm. Throwing his arms forward, stroking the water backwards, he swam a distance and deliberately looked back. Nagaveni was at the water's edge waving at him and asking him to return. Hardening his heart, Krishnayya ignored her and swam on. When he turned again, Nagaveni was not at the spot. Her head was bobbing in the water.

'Naguuuu!' he shouted swimming back as fast as he could.

Ganapayya had got up with a start when he heard Nagaveni scream, 'Krishnayyaaa!' and had run out of the house. Wondering why she had screamed, he came outside. Nagaveni was running on the road to Aralagodu.

He shut the door behind him and followed his wife. He had known things would get out of hand. He now decided he would take a decision, one way or the other. He climbed Sita Parvatha, got down the other side, came to the water farther away from where Nagaveni was and like a passive spectator, watched the scene playing out before him. Krishnayya was swimming away. Nagaveni was standing at the edge, crying hysterically and calling out to him.

Ganapayya hid behind a tree and watched, mesmerized.

Nagaveni shouted for Krishnayya. When he did not heed her pleading cry, Nagaveni jumped into the water.

Ganapayya rushed forward. He saw Krishnayya swimming speedily towards her. For a few minutes, they seemed to struggle, tossing and splashing water upwards. And then there was nothing. The water was still and brooding as it had always been.

Ganapayya did not know whether to cry or to laugh. Should he jump into the water and look for them? Or should he jump into the water and go their way?

He walked back home deep in thought.

As he stepped on to the veranda, he thought he heard a growl. He looked up. It was the tiger.

It sat crouched with its forepaws pressed to the floor and its tail thumping it. It yawned once, licked the air, and looked at Ganapayya hungrily; desiring him.

'Grr,' it growled again. Ganapayya pulled back with great effort the foot he had put forward. The tiger blinked once and stretched. Then, pressing its feet to the floor, it leapt.

Ganapayya opened his mouth to scream.

Water from the Sharavathi continued to girdle the land. The wind from Sita Parvatha continued to blow as it always did during the monsoon. And the Aslesha rain poured as usual without stopping for breath.

The maley-nakshathras that had brought in the monsoon for the year saw it to its end as usual; from *krithika* all the way to *mogge ... ubba ... utthare ... hastha ... chittha*.

***

Glossary

bewarsi	orphan
channamane,	
pagade	indoor games
chembu	a small round metal vessel
gurudakshine	a gift to the teacher
Hasalaru	the community to which the labourers, Hala and Byra belonged
habba	festival
happala	rice crispies
maunji	a girdle made of munja grass
Mirugi	a colloquial term for Mrigashira
moksha	spiritual release
odyana	waist-belt; girdle

pani-panche	a short strip of cloth men tie around the waist while bathing
panche	a length of cloth men wear around the waist to cover the lower part of the body
parvatha	mountain
pinda	rice offering made during the annual ritual for the dead
raavu	demon
sunna	quicklime
vaidya	doctor who uses herbal medicines to treat his parents

Krithika, Rohini, Mrigashira, Aridhraa, Punarvasu, Pushya, Aslesha, Mogge, Ubba, Utthara, Hastha, and Chittha are stars that influence the different phases of the monsoon.

About the Author and

the Translator

Author

NA. D'SOUZA was born in Shimoga district Karnataka. He worked in Public Works Department, Government of Karnataka for 35 years. His interests are reading, writing, travelling, and participating in activities concerning the environmental. He began writing at the age of 21 and has published forty-five novels, the most famous being *Manjina Kanu*, *Dweepa*, and *Baman*. Many of his short stories and novels have been translated into Telugu, Malayalam, Tamil, Sanskrit, Konkoni, Hindi, and English.

He has been honoured with many awards and received an honorary doctorate for his literary work from Kuvempu University and the Sahitya Akademi Bal Puraskar in 2011. The year 2012 brought the Bala Sahitya Puraskar for *Mulugade Urige Bangavan* from the Sahitya Akademi. Two of his novels *Dweepa* and *Kadina Benki* have been produced as films by well-known directors, Girish Kasaravalli and Suresh Heblikar.

Translator

SUSHEELA PUNITHA was born in Bangalore, Karnataka. She is a former Professor of English, Mount Carmel College, and Centre for Postgraduate Studies, Seshadripuram College, Bangalore. She has written stories for rural children for a UNICEF project called *Children for Change* and has translated Vaidehi's *Vasudeva's Family: Aspruhsyaru* (OUP 2012) and U.R. Ananthamurthy's *Bharathipura* (2011) which was short-listed for both The Hindu Literary Prize and the DSE Prize for South Asian Literature in 2011.